POOR GIRL'S HOPE

HISTORICAL VICTORIAN SAGA

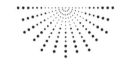

DOLLY PRICE

PUREREAD.COM

CONTENTS

1. Honest Work   1
2. In Sickness and In Health   23
3. The Sins of the Father   41
4. Maids and Ladies   67
5. A Medical Man   88
6. In Writing   105
7. Ashes to Ashes   127
8. An Ill Wind   153
9. The High Road   165

Love Victorian Romance?   179
Our Gift To You   181

HONEST WORK

"It is true, I'm afraid," said the lawyer, Mr Quigley. "Your husband has left very little. It seems that, in the past few months, he got into difficult straits, and was intending to meet one of his creditors when he rode out and had his—er—fatal fall..."

The lawyer stopped short, sensing that this might be a difficult subject. Mrs Abbott had sat down hard in her chair and did not speak for a few moments. When she lifted her head to look at him again, the tears glinted in her eyes but did not fall; it was as though her face had turned to marble and refused them passage.

"He never told me," she said, angrily.

Mr Quigley blinked. He was well-accustomed to grieving widows and knew how to adjust the modulations of his voice to soothe their tears. But feminine anger alarmed him; he didn't quite know what to do with it. He thought he ought to let a little silence fall between them to allow Mrs Abbott time to gather herself. Perhaps he would look around the room, and pretend to be interested in the furnishings?

But that was a mistake. No sooner had Mr Quigley let his eyes fall on the pretty embroidery on the worktable than he found something else to alarm him: a small movement, out of the corner of his eye. With a quick glance, he turned to the black curtains that were closed over the bow window, and whose material twitched as though by the movement of a hand. How ghostly was the house of one recently dead! The curtains went still a moment later, but he thought he heard a soft exhalation, as close as though it had been right in his ear.

"I am sure," he said quickly, directing his gaze back to Mrs Abbott, "I am sure your husband did not want to give you unnecessary worry. No doubt he hoped to have the mess cleared up before it came to your attention. Of course, he could not have predicted—he could not have expected the accident that—er—befell him..." Here he was, veering into dangerous waters once more. He coughed to hide his confusion.

"If he didn't wish to give me unnecessary worry," said Mrs Abbott, her voice bitter, "then he shouldn't have borrowed more than he could afford."

"Ah! Well, if only it were that simple, my dear Mrs Abbott." Mr Quigley was at his ease once more. "But even honest men do have their temptations, you know, and—"

He never got the chance to finish his assertion, which, no doubt, would have been thoroughly relevant and appropriate, as a child emerged from behind the black curtains, exclaiming, "It isn't true! It isn't!"

Mr Quigley could not help recoiling a little. The child looked somewhere between five years old and ten; it was difficult to tell for sure, for curtains of straw-coloured hair obscured most of her face. Her eyes, ringed and puffy, stared out at him from between the strands.

"Demelza, you're a very wicked girl," said Mrs Abbott, rising at once and going to her daughter. "I have told you before how wrong it is to eavesdrop on conversations that do not concern you."

"But he... he..." gasped the child, her eyes flickering over again to Mr Quigley. He had risen with Mrs Abbott, and watched her warily, with the air of a man compiling a defence against an eloquent enemy. But before she could get the rest of her accusation out, her mother smoothed back her fair hair from her forehead and silenced her with a look.

"Get a candle from Morris and go back to bed. Go on."

The child departed with a sniff, and the mother, after a moment's deliberation, followed after her. There was a brief, undignified conference out in the passage with the servant. Raised voices reached Mr Quigley in the parlour, as he stood poised with one hand on his waistcoat pocket. Then finally, Mrs Abbott returned.

Esther Abbott was a good-looking woman; Mr Quigley had always observed the fine lines of her face when he saw her walking through town by her husband's side. But mourning clothes had turned mere handsomeness to beauty; standing in the doorway in the candlelight, with her face and hands thrown into sharp relief by her black crepe, she looked like a Renaissance painting.

"You must excuse my daughter, sir. She has no brothers or sisters to keep her in check, and I'm afraid I have let her run a little wild."

"She has just lost her father," Mr Quigley said, inclining his head. "I can imagine..." However, it was difficult to imagine what might be going on in any child's brain. Mr James Quigley was one of those gentlemen who saw children as a separate species and, if reminded that he himself had once been a child, would have looked astonished at the suggestion.

He looked back at Mrs Abbott and made sure to layer his next words with a significance that she could not miss. "If you should... find yourself in difficulty, at any time, I am at your service."

She did not hesitate. "Thank you, Mr Quigley. You have always been a good friend to Walter. He has left us a great many problems, but I will find my own way out of it. I will return to teaching, and support Demelza and myself in that way."

"Oh." The lawyer was unable to hide his surprise. "That is— very admirable, Mrs Abbott. I wish you the best of luck."

The servant showed him out. It was a still night. Up and down the street, parlour windows were ablaze, so that Mr Quigley seemed to pass from light to shadow as he walked up the pavement. But when he reached Walter Abbott's old warehouse, its windows were black. He rummaged in his pocket, produced a key, and climbed the steps into its dark depths.

Demelza Abbott was ten years old, and not five, though Mr Quigley could be excused for thinking that she was younger. She was small in stature and moved about with a sort of loping run that was not usually observed in little girls her age. She was shy of strangers, but bold within the bounds of her own home, where, until recently, she had indeed been allowed to "run a little wild". But that was not Mrs Abbott's fault, despite what she had suggested to Quigley. It was entirely due to the indulgence of the girl's father.

The Abbotts' other children had died in infancy, and when Demelza was born, she did not seem likely to outlive them. Pale and puny, she seemed designed to bring only more disappointment to her parents, and Esther Abbott, whose heart had been hardened by one loss after another, turned her face away from the child and handed her over to her father.

Mr Abbott's hopes had already been dangerously raised by the encouraging words of the midwife, and with each new day that found his little Demelza alive and well, those hopes grew and grew. He had always wished for a son, but he was enthralled by this new daughter, who watched him with solemn eyes as though he were the most important being on earth. When she was old enough, he used to take her to the warehouse, and she would sit in the corner of his office with a doll, while he met with important men who talked about profit margins and weekly revenues. His colleagues learned not to question the constant presence of the child.

It was said during those first few years of Demelza's life, as she was often sick, that Walter Abbott had kept her alive through sheer force of will. He seemed so grateful for her continued existence that he could not imagine laying down any rules to govern it, and so it fell to Esther to try and counter-act the influence of a doting father. Of course, it was no use. Demelza did not pay her mother much mind. Why should she, when her father gave her all the adoration and care that she needed? It was all the more baffling, then, to the child, when at the age of eight, her father suddenly seemed to withdraw from her, closing the door between them and shutting her out of his bright, busy world.

Demelza did what any other child would have done in the circumstances, who had never been kept on the margins of anything before. She refused to be locked out. She sneaked into the warehouse and listened in on conversations that did not concern her. And it was for this reason that she began to form a suspicion of the lawyer.

Mr Quigley hadn't really done anything to earn this suspicion. But Demelza saw how he always seemed to bring her father bad news; she sometimes glimpsed, through the half-open door, her father's head sinking down onto his desk after Mr Quigley had left. And so, a week after her father's death, when Mr Quigley came to their house bringing the worst news of all, Demelza could not believe that it was true. She could not imagine her father getting on a horse after drinking; she thought he could never have gotten himself into debt; he would never have left them with nothing.

"Things are going to be very different in Hazelhurst," Esther told her daughter, a few days after Mr Quigley's visit, as they were packing up their things. "You can't run about the way you used to. You will only speak when spoken to, and you must be careful not to get in anyone's way."

The words fell on Demelza's consciousness without really reaching her. Her eyes were still wet with tears, for they had just dismissed Morris, the last of their servants, and tomorrow they were giving up the house, and her father had barely been dead a fortnight—and so much change in so short a time would have been enough to make anyone's head spin. For a child whose narrow experience of life had been one of comfort and freedom, it felt like the end of the world.

And so it was, in a way: it was the end of the world as they had known it with Mr Abbott alive. Esther had been a governess before her marriage and remembered going hungry; she was therefore better prepared than her daughter to greet these new, reduced circumstances. She would have preferred to take a post much farther off than Hazelhurst Grange, of course, so that she would not have to meet her husband's friends in town and see their pitying eyes—but the Seymours were offering her a good salary, and their children were known to be well-behaved. She knew she would not find a better situation.

Demelza looked up with a kind of horror at the trees that passed over their heads as the carriage brought them into the Seymours' estate. She was not used to trees, and they seemed to hem her in. All her affection was for the chimneys and hydraulic cranes of Hartleton. She wanted to say something, to make one last, desperate attempt to dissuade her mother from bringing them here, but meeting Esther's stern glance across the carriage, she knew it would be pointless. Her mother had said, after all, that she was going to have to learn to be silent and so Demelza started practising.

It worked, for a time. The big house was so strange and new that it brought out Demelza's natural shyness. She was scared of the maids and footmen, and altogether terrified of the invisible, awesome presences that were the Seymour family. For the first few weeks following their move to the Grange, it was easy to stay out of the way, as she spent most of her time in the servants' quarters, helping the housekeeper while her mother was teaching.

She quickly made the acquaintance of the housekeeper's son, another child who spent a lot of time below stairs. Cecil was a pale, black-haired boy, only a year or two older than she was, and Demelza thought he was very clever. She had never had any friends her age before, and things always promised to be interesting with Cecil. They played all sorts of games together, sneaking around the servants' quarters on quiet summer afternoons or chasing each other around the kitchen garden. It was on one such occasion that Cecil dared Demelza to go upstairs.

"And not just to the hall, either. That's too easy. I dare you to go right into the drawing room."

They were sitting in the housekeeper's room. Mrs Simms had dozed off in her chair, a bit of unfinished knitting in her lap, and her son was watching Demelza eagerly.

"I'll get Mother in trouble, if I'm caught," she said. "I'm not supposed to go up there."

"Oh, don't tell me you're too chicken. You—"

Mrs Simms stirred in her sleep, and they both started guiltily. But Demelza, who had grabbed Cecil's arm in her fright, was clearly the more shaken of the two, and this seemed to amuse him to no end.

"I'm not chicken," she said angrily, letting go again as he began to laugh. She was starting to think he wasn't such a nice boy after all. "I'm not."

"You are. Why, you're a great baby. You're afraid of everything. Probably because you don't have your daddy to protect you anymore—"

Demelza sprang forward and grabbed Cecil by the shoulders. He stopped talking and watched her instead with eyes that were dark and alert.

"You don't talk about him," she snapped. "Don't you dare."

She thought, for a minute, that Cecil was actually scared, because he was so quiet. But then he flashed her a nasty smile. "If you're so tough, why don't you prove it?"

Demelza stared at him, her shoulders heaving up and down. "All right," she said, summoning so much venom into those two words that anyone except the insolent boy in her grip would have been alarmed. She let go of him and stormed out.

It would be easy, she told herself as she climbed the servants' stairs. Since it was Sunday, most of the servants were out, visiting their families. All she had to do was get as far as the drawing room door, and then she would turn back. It did not even occur to her to lie to Cecil, not only because it would have been dishonourable, but because something in his dark eyes told her that he would know. He really was not a nice boy at all.

She had an idea of the layout of the house above stairs, gathered from the talk of the servants. But it was bigger and grander than she had expected. Demelza was a small child, and she felt as though she were getting even smaller as she passed under the statues and paintings: she felt like an ant crawling along the walls. Every fall of her foot seemed to send its own mocking echo, and she glanced around only to find the hall stretching out empty behind her.

Demelza got to the drawing room door and put out a plump fist to touch its surface, feeling that would somehow seal the dare. But it swung inward with the motion of her hand—it had not been fully closed—and from within came a lady's voice. She was singing, and accompanying herself on the piano, punctuating the end of each verse with a flourish of notes.

It was a folk song, about betrayal and broken vows and innocent young maidens who had been used ill. Demelza did not understand those things now, but she felt the sadness of the singer, that came through in the tremble of her voice and the occasional stumble of her fingers on the keys. Somehow these imperfections added to the divinity of the performance, and Demelza stood with one hand on the door, enchanted. She had met Mrs Seymour.

Cecil had been right, though Demelza would never have admitted it to his face. There was nothing to fear. She was not punished for what she dared to do that day, and so she came back often, hiding herself in the curtains as she had often done in their old house, to listen to the lady's singing.

Often in daydreams, Demelza had conjured up for herself a different mother: a softer, gentler mother than the one she had, a mother who would never tell her that she was too old to be still playing with dolls. These daydreams had always brought with them a twinge of guilt, but they had come all the same. Now she had met that mother of her dreams. Mrs Seymour was younger than Demelza imagined a mother could be, with long red tresses like a princess from a fairytale. When Demelza learnt from one of the servants that the lady's first name was Clara, she felt a new thrill within her: it was just the sort of the name she had imagined belonged to that creature, delicate and dreamy and beautiful.

Mrs Seymour's children were beautiful, too. The son came to listen to his mother's playing more often than the daughter did, and, sometimes he would even join in. Then Demelza, from her hiding place, would see two red heads bent over the piano, and hear the layered melody played by four hands. In such moments, she was always reminded of herself and her father.

Cecil grew curious about her frequent, secret trips upstairs. Though he never told the other servants, he would often corner Demelza when she returned and ask whether she had overheard anything interesting. Once he even made a reference to Mr Seymour that was so confusing, Demelza repeated it to her mother that night.

"What?" said Esther. They had been going over French verbs; Demelza went to the local school during the week, but not trusting the educators of Hartleton parish school to arm her daughter with sufficient learning, her mother had started giving her extra lessons in the evenings. "What did that boy say to you?"

"He said the maids like cleaning the drawing room because it's the only place they're safe from the master." Demelza frowned up at her mother. "What did he mean, Mother? Is Mr Seymour very cross?"

"You're to stay away from that boy from now on," said Esther, shortly. "He's full of nonsense and filth. Now, what is the past participle of être?"

～

Mr Quigley had offered Esther Abbott his assistance should she ever need it, and his offer had been genuinely meant. After all, he and her late husband had worked closely together for close to a decade. Mr James Quigley was not a native of Hartleton, and he had a debt of gratitude to Mr Abbott for taking a chance on a young lawyer from London, when there were many others whom he might have trusted instead.

But Mr Quigley was no longer young nor new to his profession, and as such, there were many other matters occupying his mind in the months following Walter Abbott's death. He was dimly aware of the fact that Esther Abbott was now governess at Hazelhurst Grange, but as his dealings with the Seymours did not extend past an occasional meeting with their patriarch, she was not forced upon his view very often, and he had almost entirely forgotten about the existence of the child.

It was, therefore, all the more surprising when, in the last week of August, on a heavy day when the sun was hidden in banks of cloud, Walter Abbott's widow paid Mr Quigley a visit. He was deep in some documents when his housekeeper announced her.

"Mrs Abbott!" Mr Quigley scrambled to his feet, rubbing the ink from his hands as she came into the room. He straightened his glasses and shook back his fair hair. "What an unexpected pleasure. Please—do sit down. Or—perhaps—you wish to go down to the drawing room instead? I am afraid this library is not very fit for a lady. Shall we—"

"I'm no lady," said Esther Abbott, her voice low, and Mr Quigley peered at her more closely. The room was ill-lit, like every other room in this rickety old house, but he could see that she was still in mourning black, and it was difficult to tell whether that was what was making her look so pale and thin.

"My dear Mrs Abbott." His voice was gentle but firm. "I must contradict you on that point. Now, please do sit."

She obliged, setting herself in the cushioned chair he had indicated with an almost imperceptible wince. Now that she was come into the light, Mr Quigley's quick, discerning eyes caught the flecks of mud on her black boots, and he spoke with concern as he drew his chair closer to hers.

"I hope, madam, that you did not walk all the way into town?"

She bowed her head, as much as to say that she had. Mr Quigley sighed. "It is ten miles between here and the Grange, if I am not mistaken. And, you will pardon my mentioning that you look the wearier for it. I will ring for Mrs Richards to bring you some brandy—"

"Please," said the widow, raising her head suddenly, and the look in her eyes was so wild and desperate that it took him aback. "Please don't ring just yet. Please, sir, allow me to speak to you first."

Mr Quigley, who had half-risen from his chair, sat back reluctantly. "Very well," he said, regarding her more closely. It was impossible for his mind not to make comparisons between her appearance months before and her appearance now. When he had visited her after her husband's death, she had been a pillar of strength, declaring that she would stand on her own resources. Now she was faded, worn down, perhaps by her reduced status. He wondered if it was some question of money. If so, then this conversation was bound to be a difficult one. He had promised her his assistance, it was true, but an offer of assistance might take any form; it might comprise guidance, friendship, counsel; it did not have to be measured in pecuniary form.

"I am weary," said Mrs Abbott, interrupting his train of thought, "as you have said, sir. But it is not so much a weariness of body as a weariness of spirit. I—I am plagued night and day." Her voice dropped, and she did not seem able to look at him anymore. "I have endeavoured to find another situation; I have written to my brother for assistance. But it is all come to nothing. Now I come to you, Mr Quigley, asking for any protection which you can give. I—" Her head sunk into her hands, so that her face was concealed. "I fear that if I remain in Mr Seymour's employ any longer, I can no longer live with honour."

Mr Quigley had sat forward in his chair throughout her recital, his interest increasing with every word. Now he understood. She did not have to make it any more explicit; he had heard the rumours about Mr Seymour, after all, and, in some cases, had even assisted him in ensuring the silence of a maid or a farmer's wife.

"I am sorry," he said quietly to Mrs Abbott, who still had her head in her hands. "that... the gentleman of whom you speak... has not shown you the respect that you deserve."

He was much impressed with this noble sentiment of his, and even more impressed with the discreet manner in which he had communicated it. But she was not, as it soon became clear. Esther Abbott lifted her head to look at him. She was flushed, but her eyes were dry.

"I am not so sure, sir, that Mr Seymour believes I deserve any respect. I am just the same to him as any servant now. He does not care who my husband was."

Mr Quigley itched to correct her. He hated to let an inaccuracy such as that go unchecked, for, after all, he knew that Mrs Abbott would not have gotten the post as governess in the first place if not for who her husband had been. But he also knew that a lady in distress was naturally a little illogical, and so he let it slide.

"Have you spoken to his... ah..."

"To Mrs Seymour? Goodness, no." Mrs Abbott's eyes had gone wide at the idea. "I imagine that lady suffers enough already. You know that he has—pursued—many others before me?"

"Yes, I do." Mr Quigley bowed his head sadly. "And I am, of course, ready to give any assistance that you need."

"Could you speak to him?" As the lawyer hesitated, she added quickly, "Or perhaps you could write, instead? Or—or better still speak to someone who might hold some sway with him?"

"I would happily undertake to do any of those things." The gears in Mr Quigley's head were turning fast. He was not an impulsive man, but a solution had just occurred to him: one which would involve little expense on his part, and which could only serve to honour and elevate her. "However, if you will allow it, Mrs Abbott—Esther—I can offer you a greater protection than that."

Esther stared at him. Mr Quigley reached out and gently took her hand in his. He then spoke at some length about being in a certain place in his profession, about being at a certain age, that age when a man knew he was not young anymore; he spoke of his great respect for Esther, a respect that had deepened into admiration over his long acquaintance with her late husband, and that might yet deepen into love, if she gave him a chance.

She listened and sat in silence when he had finished speaking. But she did not withdraw her hand from his.

Esther and Demelza did not live in the big house with the other servants, but in a cabin at the other side of the wood that bordered the estate. It had belonged to the gamekeeper before he took larger lodgings; it had a stove that smoked and there were strange rustlings at night, but it suited their purposes. Demelza, however, had not yet conquered her dread of trees, and on that heavy summer's evening, she faced a solitary walk back to the cabin with not a little trepidation. Her mother had not returned from town yet.

It ought to have been dark, but the sun had not set, and the whole world was filled with a sickly kind of light. Cecil Simms caught up with her as she was going down the drive. "Where have you been?"

"In the scullery," said Demelza, without looking at him. "Helping Martha."

"Oh, that's why your hands are all red." His laugh grated on her nerves.

"You could try it, you know. Helping Mr Jackson or the footmen instead of making trouble all day."

"Only a fool would work for free." Cecil seemed entirely unaffected by her disapproval. "Besides, my mum wouldn't like it. She's got bigger plans for me."

This gave Demelza the opening she needed. The two children had nearly reached the wood now. With a glance back at the house, whose mullioned windows shone too bright in the light of the setting sun, she said, "My mother doesn't want me to play with you anymore."

"Oh, really?"

"Yes," said Demelza, facing towards the dark trees again. She felt a cold drop on her forehead. "So you'd better not follow me anymore."

Cecil's hand closed around her arm as she made to step away, tightening painfully. Suddenly his pale face was right up close to hers. "Who are you, then, to turn up your nose at me? Who's your mother? I've heard things about her, you know. I've heard she's been seen with the master, all alone. They say she's earning her wages in more ways than one."

Demelza didn't know what he meant, but it sounded horrible. She strained away from his grip, as more raindrops began to fall, striking the leaves with a gentle ping ping. She managed to get a little way down the wood path before Cecil came up behind her, catching a chunk of her hair in his hand and pulling her back with a painful wrench to her scalp.

"I'll tell them," he snapped. "I'll tell them you've been sneaking up there every day to listen to the mistress playing. Your mother won't be happy with you then, will she?"

"Please don't," gasped Demelza; there were tears in her eyes. The sound of the rain was rising, from a hiss to a roar. As Cecil relented, letting go of her hair, she stamped on his foot and took off into the wood.

Brambles tugged at her black dress and caught in her loose hair. She picked up the hem of her skirt and ran. She could hear him following close behind at first: sometimes his shouts drifted after her, though they began to grow fainter. Her heartbeat climbed to her throat, then to her ears, pulsing and throbbing. Every now and then, her foot would catch on some stone or twig on the path below, and she would have to throw out her hands for balance.

When she got into the clearing with their cabin, Demelza broke free from the trees and stumbled to the door without looking back. She fumbled in her pocket for the key her mother had given her. The rain was coming down hard now, and rich smells were rising from the damp soil. The sky above the treetops was cold metal grey. In the trees behind her, she could hear the crack of twigs and the rustle of bushes as her pursuer drew closer.

Mother had told her often enough, since they had come to live here, not to let any strangers come to visit when she was not around. She never gave a reason, but now Cecil's words were sinking into Demelza's mind like feet in wet soil, producing half-formed ideas and shadowy glimpses of a world she did not yet understand. She found her key at last, got inside the dark safety of the cabin and did up the bolt with trembling hands.

"Hello?" A voice came from outside the door, a voice which belonged to a boy, but not to Cecil. It was slightly out of breath. Demelza had frozen at the sound; now she flew back to the door and leaned her weight against it, trying to make sure that it would not give even if the bolt did. On the other side, she heard the crunch of grass underfoot, and the swoosh of rain.

"I'm sorry if I frightened you," came the boy's voice, after a moment's pause. "I'm Nathaniel. I've wanted to talk to you for a while."

Demelza's eyes were wide now. Mrs Seymour's son—the young master, the boy with red hair—was outside, talking to her! She brought her lips close to the crack in the door, and said, "My mother told me not to let anyone in."

"That's all right," said Nathaniel. On the other side of the door, she heard him scuff his shoe on the ground. "I don't mind the rain."

Feeling a pang of conscience, Demelza deliberated for a moment, and then searched in the coat-stand for her mother's umbrella. Her heartbeat had slowed in her chest, and she was not scared anymore—she did not see how she could be scared of that boy's voice. Holding it in one hand, she unfastened the bolt with the other and then stepped out.

The boy started back a bit, surprised. Demelza's eyes darted up to take him in, and then down again. She saw, in that brief glance, that he was a few years older than her: that the red curls she had noticed before were pressed close to his head, dripping from the rain; that his eyes were a very pale blue, and had none of the dark watchfulness of Cecil's. A dusting of freckles on the boy's nose made him look all the friendlier.

Demelza struggled with the clasp of her mother's umbrella. Every now and then it would give and then slide back, and finally it opened, just in time for a rogue gust of wind to snap it inside out. She cried out in dismay, while the older boy laughed.

"I don't see what's so funny," she said resentfully, with another darting glance at him from under her curtain of hair. "Mother will have to buy a new one now."

"I can fix it. Here." The boy reached out and took the umbrella, and as he was concentrating on his task, Demelza looked at him again, and began to feel a little more relaxed. She didn't even mind the rain so much either—not when something so very interesting was happening. But there was one point on which she still needed to be satisfied.

"Is Cecil still coming?" she asked the boy, and he shook his head as he opened the umbrella, propping it above their heads.

"I chased him off."

"I thought you were him at first," Demelza said, by way of explanation. "That's why I didn't stop, when you shouted. He was so cross."

"I saw him teasing you," said Nathaniel, and suddenly he looked very serious. "I told him a boy his age should leave little girls like you alone."

"I'm not so little," said Demelza, indignantly. "I'll be eleven next March."

Nathaniel chose—wisely—not to diminish the grandeur of eleven. He himself was fourteen, and would be going away to school soon. The last true summer of his childhood was over, and now here this child stood before him, more fairy than girl, with her fine blonde hair and pointed ears: it was like she had stepped out of one of his storybooks to remind him of what he was about to leave behind.

"I've seen you," he said, thoughtfully. "In the drawing room, hiding behind the curtain when my mother's singing. Do you like singing?"

Demelza had gone bright red: she hung her head, her old shyness returning.

"I like when she sings," she mumbled.

"It's all right." Nathaniel had noticed her embarrassment and seemed anxious to remedy it. "We don't mind. We've always known you were there, but my mother told me not to say anything to scare you off. She thinks you're very sweet."

Another question came to Demelza now, through her embarrassment, and there was something in Nathaniel's kind manner which made her think he might answer it. But when she asked, "Why are her songs always so sad?" and glanced up anxiously for his response, a shadow fell over the older boy's face.

In her innocence, Demelza had not expected to give offence; she was thinking of her own father, and the way he had withdrawn from her during the last couple of years of his life. She had never learnt what had made him so sad, although she had her suspicions. Maybe if she had known, she would have been able to help. The same reasoning had prompted her question about Mrs Seymour, but she saw quickly that she had made a mistake.

Nathaniel glanced up at the grey sky, determinedly avoiding her gaze. "I'd better get back. It's nearly suppertime." He made to hand her back the umbrella, but Demelza shook her head, stepping out of its circle.

"It's still raining," she said shyly. "You should keep it."

He thanked her and made for the trees. She slipped back to the door, half-hiding herself behind it, and watched him from the threshold. When he had gone a little way, Nathaniel turned back and said, his voice barely audible over the rain, "I'm glad I met you."

There was a finality to his tone which confused Demelza. Change was a foreign thing to her, and like many children, she did not think about the future. In her mind, Nathaniel would always be there in the drawing room, playing duets with his mother. She did not realise that it would be a long time before she and her new friend met again. So she smiled, but was silent, and lingered in the door after Nathaniel Seymour had disappeared.

A familiar step coming through the trees soon caught her attention, and her mother emerged into the clearing a moment or two after Nathaniel had departed, carrying an umbrella that was not her own. She gazed at Demelza with a kind of exasperated astonishment, and said as she came up, "Was that the young master I saw, just leaving?"

"Yes," said Demelza, a little ashamed, and then, hastily, "He's very nice, Mother. He said he'd wanted to meet me for a while."

"I've told you not to let anyone in when I'm not home."

"But he didn't come in, we just stood outside and talked—"

"Well, never mind now. Come and sit down, I have something important to tell you." Esther Abbott closed the door behind them and took off her cloak. She poked the red ashes of the fire that had been set earlier in the day, and then beckoned her daughter over. There was an odd, wary look in her face, and yet she looked younger too; there was a flush to her cheek and a brightness to her eye. Years later, Demelza would always remember how her mother looked that evening.

But she did not remember the exact words her mother used to introduce the idea of her second marriage, or the manner in which she described the worthiness of Mr Quigley. Probably, at the time, she did not really hear her; probably, she was only aware of the great chasm that was, once again, opening up beneath her: she only felt, once again, the end of the world as she knew it.

The next morning, Demelza went with her mother into Hartleton to meet the man who was soon to be her stepfather. When Nathaniel came to the cabin to return the umbrella, he saw that the windows were dark, and no one answered his knock. He was in a hurry; back in the house, his things were already packed, and the servant and carriage waiting to take him away, his mother waiting to kiss him goodbye.

He left the umbrella propped up against the wall of the cabin, its end dripping onto the steps. He was conscious at the time of a faint disappointment that he would not see Demelza again, but he would soon forget her and the whole episode. He went away, and the umbrella dried in the sun.

2

IN SICKNESS AND IN HEALTH

Six years later, a carriage was toiling up a steep lane in Hartleton when its wheels got stuck in the mud and caused it to overturn.

The more agile of the carriage's inhabitants got out first, a pale young woman, and she helped her older companion out. There was much outcry on this lady's part, though, thankfully, neither of them had been injured. All the noise attracted a few haymakers from the fields nearby, and they came up to confer with the driver, and then to check that the ladies were all right.

"All right?!" repeated Mrs Aldridge, pressing one hand to her heart as though the expression wounded her. "We might have been killed!"

"I was going so slow, ma'am, that it hardly seems likely," defended the driver, which by no means reassured Mrs Aldridge. One of the farmhands then remarked that if they were Hartleton bound, they ought to have stayed on the high road, and the driver was on the point of agreeing with the man when Mrs Aldridge gave an indignant huff.

"I beg your pardon, but we are not going to Hartleton proper: we are going to my brother Quigley's house. He lives just over that hill. Now, how else would you suggest we reach it if not for this lane?"

Her question had been posed rhetorically, but in answering it, the outspoken farmhand embarked on a very sensible explanation as to how they would go about getting to Highfield House without risking their carriage on a lane fit only for carts. Mrs Aldridge, as she listened, was slowly turning purple. Meanwhile, a quick, involuntary smile showed on the face of the young woman, who had been silent up until now, and several of the farmhands turned to look at her.

She was small, and plainly dressed: her black bonnet and white tucker made her look a little forbidding. Her face had traces of the elfin about it, in the ears and chin, but her extreme pallor and shadowed eyes suggested that she had been recently ill. A few blond strands hung loose from her bonnet, which was the only sign of conventional prettiness about her; as it was, the men quickly lost interest.

"You might well laugh," said Mrs Aldridge, angrily, for she had not missed the young woman's brief spell of mirth either. "Oh, yes! This has been quite the holiday for you, hasn't it? But in my brother's house, you know, you will have to make yourself useful."

The young woman hung her head, and Mrs Aldridge, whose spirits seemed to have been improved by the outburst, turned back to the farmhands and addressed them with more gentility than before, informing them that she and her brother's stepdaughter had had a long journey from Bristol, and that if they could help them out of their predicament and send them off in the right direction, she would be most grateful. The men obliged, righting the carriage as the ladies stood apart, and pushing it down to the bottom of the lane. Then, after a few more exchanges with the driver, the men headed back into the fields.

"How disagreeable!" said Mrs Aldridge. "We shall have to walk now to meet it. Let me hold onto your arm, Demelza, I feel rather faint."

Demelza Abbott, who was out of breath herself, was nevertheless in the habit of obeying Mrs Aldridge, and so she held out her arm and let the older lady lean her considerable weight on her. They walked down the steep lane toward where the carriage was waiting, Mrs Aldridge grumbling all the while, her hoop skirt swaying back and forth and, at intervals, striking at the backs of Demelza's legs. The tracks of the men's shoes ran before them in the mud, which was another point of contention with Mrs Aldridge, who, unlike her younger companion, was wearing a lilac gown that showed up stains much more clearly.

There were some advantages after all, Demelza reflected, to being in mourning.

Mr James Quigley had purchased Highfield House after his marriage. Once a farmhouse, Highfield had been expanded by its previous inhabitants to make it fit for a gentleman's abode. It had pointed gables and rambling passageways. The house was well-placed, too; from the breakfast room, one could observe the steeple of Hartleton's parish church in the valley below, and the library overlooked the edges of the wood that enclosed Hazelhurst Grange.

Demelza, who had spent all of her holidays in Bristol, felt a painful revival of grief as soon as their carriage pulled up outside the house. But she did not have long for contemplation, for they were soon surrounded, the gravel of the approach crunching underfoot: Mr and Mrs White embraced Mrs Aldridge each in turn, overflowing with eager inquiries; their daughter Gertrude looked Demelza up and down before going to greet her aunt; and Mr Quigley was the last to emerge from the door, taking his time coming down the steps.

He shook Demelza's hand in grave silence. He was much older than when she had last seen him, his shock of fair hair had turned white, and small, dark eyes peered out from behind round spectacles. "We were expecting you sooner," was his only remark, and this was quickly answered by Mrs Aldridge, who embarked on an account of their journey which carried them indoors and which garnered her much sympathy from her brother and sister.

Demelza, it seemed, was exempt from this sympathy, but she was not really surprised, and accepted her role with not a little relief; it would have been far worse, she reasoned to herself, to have been pressed with questions when all she really wanted was to be alone. Between herself and the sullen maid (none of the other servants were to be found, which was not really surprising either), the luggage was divided and carried upstairs, most of it ending up in the guest room that had been assigned to Mrs Aldridge. Demelza then proceeded up to the third floor with her own battered suitcase, to get changed.

The gable room had not been used in a long time, and most of its furniture had been covered in dust sheets. She removed these one by one and forced the stiff latch of the window open. The evening air drifted in, bringing with it the sound of the church bells, and the chattering voices of the maids, whose room was directly above Demelza's.

At dinner, Mrs Aldridge continued the account of their journey. "Our driver was really most impertinent. And it was his taking us up that cart lane that caused us to overturn. Wasn't it, Demelza?"

"Yes, Mrs Aldridge," said Demelza, who knew better than to contradict that lady—but Mrs White, watching her avidly, pounced upon her answer.

"You really ought not to be so formal, Demelza. I can understand it when you were at school—but now you are at home, among your family. We are really your aunts, you know, and some people might find it strange, to see that you are so formal."

Demelza apologised, but Mrs White and Mrs Aldridge were not satisfied until they had heard the words 'Aunt Josephine' and 'Aunt Agnes' pronounced by her lips. Then Mr White added, most generously, that she might call him 'Uncle Geoffrey'. Mr Quigley was silent. Demelza was grateful for that. He had done his share of injustices to her, including marrying her mother, but at least he had never demanded that she call him 'Father'.

"I hope," Mrs White went on, addressing Demelza but looking at the others seated at the table, "that you have learned a great deal at Agnes's school. I understand you were most troublesome at first."

"Oh! Most troublesome," declared Mrs Aldridge with a new enthusiasm, for her sister had just introduced her favourite subject. "She tried to run away, you know. More than once."

"That was in my first year, aunt." Demelza was willing to surrender on some fronts, but she felt that Mrs Aldridge's account was missing some important details. "I was still a child, and I was homesick."

"Homesick! You ought to have been grateful. Not every young girl like yourself would have had such an opportunity for education. In any case," Mrs Aldridge turned back to her brother and sister, "it is true that she is more well-behaved now. But what you see before you is the fruit of four years' labour."

They all studied Demelza for a moment.

"She's very small and pale," said Mr White, thoughtfully. "Not like our Gertrude."

For comparison, all eyes turned to the dark-haired and rose-cheeked Gertrude, who smiled demurely at her plate.

"That's because she was ill, I expect," said Mrs White, her tone suggesting that this was some failing on Demelza's part. "Weak constitution, like her mother, I suppose. I always thought Esther didn't get enough exercise. I told her often, but she was too much the fine lady after her marriage, too much at home. You need not fear, Demelza; we will give you plenty of errands here, to get you out and about."

Demelza's hands were trembling so hard that she could not hold her fork steady and had to set it down.

"What a fright Demelza gave us!" Mrs Aldridge exclaimed, shaking her head at the recollection. "We lost three other girls, you know, in the outbreak."

"Poor little souls," said Mrs White, piously.

"And such a lot of work goes into three funerals—you can't imagine. With the school under quarantine, it all fell on our shoulders. It would have been most inconvenient to have a fourth. And there was a talk of another inspector coming, you know—very unpleasant. But that's all over now."

"May I ask, Demelza," said Mr Quigley, speaking for the first time since the start of dinner—she chanced a glance toward him, and saw the hints of a smile on his face, "If you are still in the habit of eavesdropping on conversations that do not concern you?"

"No, sir," she said, quietly.

"Then I commend you, Agnes." He raised his glass of wine towards his sister. "You have certainly improved her."

~

The last time Demelza had been caught eavesdropping, which was, undoubtedly, the time to which her stepfather had been referring at dinner, it had resulted in her being sent away to school.

She was twelve by then, and her mother had been married to Mr Quigley for almost two years. The Whites had moved in and were directing everything; Mr White was running Demelza's father's old business, with Mr Quigley's help, and Mrs White took her place as lady of the house, a responsibility apparently deemed too great for her sister-in-law. Esther was relegated to governess once more and spent most of every day in the stuffy schoolroom with Gertrude and Demelza.

Demelza often wondered, in those days, what Esther had gotten out of the arrangement with Mr Quigley. She thought of it as an arrangement rather than a marriage, because she seldom saw a warm word pass between them. Yet her mother seemed content, or, if not content, at least at peace: the shadow that had hung over her at the Grange was passed. But a new shadow was creeping over Demelza. She had, for the first time, the sense of being replaced.

Gertrude was everything that she wasn't. She was clever where Demelza was dull; she was graceful where her step-cousin was clumsy; she was dutiful where the other girl was outspoken. And, more and more, Demelza began to see that her mother's smiles were reserved for Gertrude; her warm praise seldom reached her own daughter.

It was, therefore, for her own selfish reasons that Demelza hid behind the curtains in the drawing room one day, after lessons were over. She had a child's spiteful need to hear ill of herself; she wanted to know who was saying what, so that she could carve out a new, bitter grudge against them in her heart. What she ended up hearing instead was something she could never have imagined.

Her mother and Mr Quigley came in, shutting the door behind them, and it quickly became clear that Demelza had caught them in the middle of an argument. Their voices were hushed but intense, and as they drew nearer to her hiding place, she was able to make out the words.

"... deny you anything, James," her mother was saying. "But it's too painful, don't you understand? I can't bear to go through it again."

"Has it crossed your mind, my dear, that there are some things more important than your own wishes?" Mr Quigley's voice was cool and measured, as it always was, but there was just a hint of savage humour to it that set goosebumps on Demelza's skin. "And do you recall that when I asked you to marry me, it was with the understanding that the benefit would not be all on your side?"

"Of course! But—" Demelza's mother's voice rose a fraction, and she hastily lowered it again, evidently at some sign given by her husband. "Forgive me, my dear, I will be tranquil. But you must know, James, that I want what you want. I have

30

always wanted a son. But God gave me only Demelza—and I think—I fear—that he will not give me another child. I fear that if I keep trying, I will... I will..."

She didn't finish her thought, but took a quick breath as though holding back a sob. Demelza was frozen; she had never seen her mother cry before. A long, heavy silence followed, during which Demelza heard her stepfather's quick, agitated footsteps, as though he were pacing the room. At length he said, with forced brightness, "Well, my dear. You needn't look so tragic. After all, perhaps the fault lies with me. Perhaps it is simply that I am not so great a man as your last husband."

"That's not—"

"You may be excused, my dear. Since it is now evident to me that this marriage brings you nothing but pain, I would not want to make you suffer any longer with my presence—"

"Oh, James..."

"Out! Get OUT!"

Demelza moved as soon as she heard him shout. Instinct drove her out from behind the curtain to interrupt the awful scene, and she was made of pure fury as she cried, "Don't touch her!"

Mr Quigley had a hand at her mother's throat, and his face was white and close to hers. He was breathing hard. Slowly, he turned his gaze on Demelza, let go of Esther, and brushed his hand on his waistcoat as though it had been sullied by the contact. Esther did not look at her daughter. Her head was lowered, tears running down her face.

The next day, Mr Quigley's sister in Bristol was written to, and it was settled that Demelza would be sent away.

James Quigley was not the sort of man who had any illusions about himself. He was not blind to his own faults; his manner of living his life was more like that of a horse with blinkers. He saw what he needed to see and ignored the rest. But of course, there were moments when the blinkers fell away, and those moments had been coming more frequently since his wife's death.

On the day of Demelza's return to Hartleton, he had one such moment. All that talk about illness and weak constitutions at dinner certainly hadn't helped, and as Mr Quigley was watching the ladies withdraw from the dining room, his gaze fell on his stepdaughter, and he saw in her bowed head, in the slight tremble in her hands as she folded them behind her back, something of her mother's attitude. The girl, of course, had been unable to come home to Esther on her sickbed, due to the outbreak in Agnes's school, and that did seem cruel. Suddenly, briefly, Mr Quigley felt shocked at himself. He felt he ought to do something, say something, though he did not know what. What had Esther said again before she died, what were those words that had sent a chill through him? *I will pray for you.*

And then the moment passed, and his brother-in-law came up to hand him his snuffbox, and Mr Quigley took it and asked him calmly how the plan was going.

"The plan—the plan?" Mr White looked thrown for a moment. He was a short man, with a florid countenance and long hair at the sides of his head that sprouted off his baldness on top. "Oh, you mean Josephine's plan to get the young people together." He laughed. "Quite well, I understand. They are calling on the Grange tomorrow, on the pretext of helping Miss Seymour with the preparations for her coming-out. But of course, it is the young man they are going for. And I'm sure he will take to Gertrude."

"Yes, there is no doubt about that." Mr Quigley smiled; his uneasy mood from moments before was evaporated, forgotten. "It will be a good thing, to have a pretty girl like Gertrude married."

"Yes, yes indeed." His brother-in-law laughed again, and this time Quigley noticed a nervous quality to his laughter. He cocked his head, turning to face him fully.

"What is it, Geoffrey?"

"Well, nothing really, only..." Mr White coughed. "Only I thought I'd better mention, Jorkins visited the warehouse again today."

Mr Quigley was silent, tapping his fingers against his snuffbox. Mr White went on, "He was anxious for a meeting with me. I got my secretary to make excuses, naturally, but then he said he just wanted to have a look around, and I didn't see how we could hinder him from that..."

"Easily, Geoffrey: easily. You have him escorted out, you tell him he is intruding upon private property. That man is a pest —there's more, isn't there?"

As Mr Quigley stared at him, White licked his lips nervously. "Well, yes. I've heard he's been taken on by the Seymours."

"Taken on? In what capacity?"

"To make improvements to the estate—a land agent, I warrant, or something of that description..."

Mr Quigley threw down his snuffbox and strode to the door of the dining room.

"W—where are you going, James? It's not so very serious, is it?"

With one hand on the door, Quigley threw a pitying glance back at his brother-in-law. "It is very serious, Geoffrey. And now there are certain things I must think about. Undisturbed. Make my excuses to the ladies."

Demelza was relieved to be free of her stepfather's presence after dinner, so that it did not occur to her to question it when Mr White came into the drawing room alone. She was able to escape to a quiet corner of the drawing room with Mrs Aldridge's sewing box and resume work on the set of the handkerchiefs she had begun last week. It was the first piece of work she had taken up since her recovery, and her hands were still a little clumsy.

At the other end of the room, Gertrude was picking out a tune on the piano, and occasionally attempting to match it with her voice, which was slightly off-key. Mrs Aldridge, arms folded, tapped out a beat with her fingers as she watched her niece fondly. Nearby, Mr and Mrs White were conferring with their heads close together, and it was only when the latter raised her voice that a snatch of their conversation reached Demelza's ears.

"It's not as though it's your fault! That man was supposed to have left after the funeral!"

"Well, unfortunately, he's still in Hartleton, and now he's been poking his nose around the warehouse—"

"It's James's mess, I'm sure, and not yours. You ought to stand up for yourself more, Geoffrey. That man—"

"What man?" said Mrs Aldridge, twitching around from her comfortable seat with some interest.

"Hugh Jorkins, Agnes," her sister informed her, in a stage-whisper. "Remember I wrote that he had come for Esther's funeral? Well, now—"

But at this juncture, Mr White laid a warning hand on his wife's arm, nodding toward the corner where Demelza sat, listening intently. They all looked in her direction, and Mrs Aldridge said sharply,

"Demelza! What do you think you're doing? You know a young girl like yourself can't afford to sit idle when there's work to be done!"

"I'm sorry, Aunt Agnes," Demelza said automatically, reaching for her needle again, but Mrs Aldridge bulled over her,

"Make yourself useful and fetch The Pickwick Papers from my room. I have a fancy for reading tonight."

Demelza rose from her chair just as Gertrude finished her piece, to a round of clapping from her fond relatives. She passed out of the room, looking back once to see that the Whites and Mrs Aldridge were deep in conversation again. Her mind was reeling, and she moved like one in a daze; had she heard them right? Was Hugh Jorkins back?

She had never met Uncle Hugh; he had left for India before she was born. Her mother had only mentioned him a few times. Demelza supposed that when someone was so far away, their concerns became distant, too. Had he come back for her mother's funeral? she wondered as she climbed the spiral staircase. Had he known Esther was ill? She felt a jealous twist of her heart; it was not fair, after all, that she had been unable to go to her own mother's funeral, but that her mother's brother, who had not seen her in almost twenty years, could come back just as he liked...

"Whoa."

Demelza had run headlong into a servant at the top of the stairs, and almost lost her balance; he put his hands on her shoulders, righting her. Then he looked her up and down and smiled unpleasantly. "Well, well. You haven't changed much, little Demi."

Demelza's eyes darted from the black hair, now neatly slicked back, to the dark, watchful eyes, the mouth quirked in a half-grin and the white, starched collar. "Neither have you," she managed to respond.

"Oh really?" said Cecil Simms, still grinning as he backed her a few steps down the corridor. "But I'm told I've grown into quite a handsome fellow. Is that true?"

"You shouldn't believe everything your mother tells you," Demelza said, with a quick glance backward. The corridor was dimly lit, and she did not know what lay at the end of it; it was too long since she had been in this house.

"Careful." Cecil's grin had vanished, and with a quick manoeuvre he had her locked against the wall with his arms on either side of her. "I'm Mr Quigley's valet now, you know. And I could make things quite unpleasant for you."

"I thought you had bigger ambitions. Didn't you always say that, when we were children?" Demelza struggled to keep her breathing steady, and met his gaze even as he leaned in. She was not a little girl anymore, after all; she had met men like him in Bristol, and she knew that what they usually wanted was to make a woman frightened or uncomfortable. "But look at you. You're still a servant."

Cecil released her, with a grimace. "And what about you?" he snapped, but there was not as much venom behind his words, as though he had lost heart. "You haven't got a penny, and you're not pretty enough to marry into money. You'll end up a governess just like your mother."

"At least I won't have to clean up other people's messes," she shot back, and Cecil's dark eyebrows rose.

"You know, Demi," he said, after a moment's pause, "I think perhaps you have changed. You're not nearly as nice as you used to be. Why is that, I wonder?"

"I grew up," she told him, and then someone coughed and they both turned to see that Gertrude had come up the stairs behind them.

"Miss White," said Cecil. His entire attitude had changed in a matter of seconds; his spine stiffened, his chin lifted, and a bland smile twisted his lips.

Gertrude was looking between them, undisguised curiosity on her face. "Cecil, do you two know one another?"

"I had the pleasure, miss, of meeting Miss Abbott at Hazelhurst Grange a few years ago," Cecil said, and then, with a bow to each of them in turn, "Do forgive my impertinence. Good evening."

He passed down the corridor and out through the baize door.

"He's an odd one, isn't he," said Gertrude, watching him go. Her eyes turned back to Demelza, and then she dimpled, very prettily. "But did he call you Demi? How sweet. I think I shall start calling you that now."

"Please don't," Demelza started to say, but the other girl had already stepped forward and looped her arm through hers.

She stood at least a head taller than Demelza.

"And you must call me Cousin Gertrude. I am determined that we should be friends. I have been wanting to get you alone since the moment you arrived, you know. There are not many other young ladies in Hartleton, and it's so tiresome to have no one to confide in." Gertrude's smile broadened as she looked at Demelza, who smiled uncertainly back.

"Aunt Agnes wanted me to fetch her a book..."

"Never mind that old battle-axe. Come on, come upstairs with me. I have the most enchanting bonnet to show you."

The bonnet in question was forgotten as soon as they got to Gertrude's room, and all the weight of the occasion afforded to her secrets instead. Gertrude sat herself down at her vanity with a flounce of fabric and directed Demelza to look out her window.

It was still light outside. From their vantage point on the hill, Demelza beheld a broad stretch of farmland below, that ran into dark woods. She frowned, feeling a stir of recognition within her. "Is that..."

"Hazelhurst, and it's all going to be mine one day," said Gertrude. She had not so much as turned from the vanity table, and let her bold statement hang on the air for a moment. Demelza straightened, turning from the window, and it was only when their gazes met in the mirror that the other girl continued,

"You're dying to know, aren't you? It's because I'm going to marry Nathaniel Seymour, you see. It's all arranged. I met him in London last season, when I had my coming-out, and he danced with me at every assembly. And he is to come into the property when he is twenty-one, you know, now that his father's dead. Oh, but I do feel so sorry for his sister. She ought to have her coming-out in town, too, like I did, but instead they insist on giving a ball in Hazelhurst. I know that Mrs Seymour doesn't like London, but why should poor Letty suffer for that?"

"Are you—" Demelza began, and her voice almost gave out. But it was only a moment's lapse, and Gertrude did not look up from arranging her hair. "Are you engaged, then, to Mr Seymour?"

But here she had hit on a sore point. Gertrude's hands dropped, and two spots of colour appeared in her cheeks. "Well, no," she said after a moment, and it sounded as though the words were being forced out of her. "He has made no offer to me yet. But Mother says it is only a matter of time— after all, it would be such a good thing for both our families, and I'm sure we should get on very well together. The difficulty is..." She sighed, her shoulders heaving. "Demi, will you fasten up these plaits for me? Then we shall go downstairs again. But I am determined not to play anymore, even if they worry me to death about it."

Demelza was too eager to hear more to voice her dislike of the nickname, although she had the uncomfortable sense that it was already being cemented into her step-cousin's vocabulary. She came forward and took the comb. "What is the difficulty?"

"Hmm?"

"About Mr Seymour."

"Oh, yes, yes. Well..." Gertrude frowned as Demelza fastened up her dark coils of hair, but in a way that was thoughtful rather than critical. "Have you ever met him?"

"No," Demelza replied right away. The lie slid easily from her lips, and at first she did not know why.

"The difficulty is that he is so good and kind to everyone. So it can be difficult, sometimes, to know what is a special attention—and what is just..."

"... him," finished Demelza, in a low voice. She took a step back, having fastened Gertrude's plaits.

"Exactly. And that is why I will need your help, Demi." Gertrude rose from her vanity table and put her hands on Demelza's shoulders, fixing her with a look of earnest appeal. "Will you come with us to Hazelhurst tomorrow? And then you can judge for yourself whether he likes me or not. And if not, then I..." She heaved a sigh. It was a sound that was full of melodrama to Demelza's ears, though her own sighs in quiet moments had probably been much the same. "... then I shall have to bear it, I suppose."

Demelza agreed. But later on, in her gable room, as she looked down at the dark valley from her window and heard carriage wheels on the town road, she wished that she had not lied to Gertrude about knowing him.

For Demelza had not forgotten Nathaniel Seymour. In that last week at Hazelhurst Grange, when everything was being arranged for her mother's marriage to Mr Quigley, she had often hoped to see her friend again. Over the next few years of her life, no happy memories came to chase Nathaniel into irrelevance. Through days in squalid schoolrooms and nights in freezing dormitories, as she heard the laboured coughs of her fellow classmates and saw the looming countenance of Mrs Aldridge, Demelza clung harder and harder to the picture in her mind, of a beautiful boy who had freckles and friendly eyes.

3

THE SINS OF THE FATHER

ugh Jorkins had not been a good brother, nor a good uncle for that matter. Growing up, he had always had the notion that he was made for great things, and shores beyond England beckoned him. Twenty years as a clerk in a trading post near Madras had fairly beaten that notion out of him. Nothing about the country suited him: the climate, the food, the strangeness of the other English who had come to settle there. Yet he stuck at it, out of sheer stubbornness, even when all possibility of promotion seemed to have worn away, and the thing that ended up bringing him back was the very thing he had endeavoured to escape from the first: his family.

Esther started writing to him a few years into her second marriage. Letters took weeks to arrive, of course, so that each time Hugh received one, he always found himself wondering what had happened in the interval between its passing out of his sister's hands and into his own. She was miserable, of course: that much was clear, though she never stated it outright. Her daughter had been sent away to her sister-in-law, she was forced to share her house with another sister-in-law and barely saw her husband anymore. Hugh formed an impression of Mr Quigley the more he read his sister's writing: the lawyer rose from the pages of script, glacial and mercenary, jealous of a shadow who was long dead and angry at his wife for being indebted to him for marrying her.

Hugh gave notice at work, gave up his accommodation and packed up to return. Esther's last letter reached him on his day of departure. He read it over and over on his long voyage home, tracing with anxiety the words that she had written of her own growing weakness, of her fear that she would not see her daughter again. By the time he reached Hartleton, she was dead.

From there, the question of where to go or what to do was no longer a pressing one. Hugh would stay on in Hartleton and find what work he could. He only needed a glimpse of his brother-in-law at Esther's funeral to know that his own impression had been true. There was more to his sister's death than a mere illness. There was something in Mr Quigley that could not be touched by love or warmth, and Hugh was going to find out what it was, even if it killed him.

This was how he found himself engaged as a land agent on the Seymours' estate, and how he happened to be mending a fence on the Kents' farm one morning when Mrs Seymour's carriage came up. Hugh instantly straightened, looking around him for anywhere that could possibly provide an escape. He had a horror of patricians, carried over from his time in India; the English there puffed themselves up so grandly and wore their titles like crowns, so that it was hard not to find those distinctions a little ridiculous now that he was returned.

But there was nowhere to escape, and no time, in any case; Mrs Clara Seymour had been handed out by a footman and was coming up the farmyard path. Hugh had spotted her at a distance before, so he was not surprised to see that she was relatively young and what some might call beautiful. It only seemed a wonder how ill she fit in with her environment: here she was, with red ringlets, a ribboned bonnet and a striped crinoline, side-stepping cowpats and muddy puddles —the contrast was a little ridiculous, and it was only with an extraordinary effort that Hugh did not laugh outright.

Instead, he took off his hat and bowed his head, his dark hair falling over his brow. "Good day, ma'am."

"Good day. Mr Jorkins, isn't it? I have business with my tenant." She sounded flat and uninterested: the sort of stiff-neck who only lit up when she was talking about horse breeding or hunting, Hugh imagined. "Have you seen Parsons?"

"No, ma'am." Mr Parsons was the land manager, whom Mrs Seymour had employed a few months ago to make improvements to her estate. Hugh was effectively apprenticed to him, which was a bit of a step down for a man of nearly forty, but then again, he had bigger concerns at the moment than his own pride. "It's just me today."

"Very good." She passed him and continued through the gate and into the Kents' yard. Hugh, after a moment's uncertainty, followed after her. She did not turn or acknowledge his presence in any other way, so he imagined she did not object to it, at the very least.

The farmstead was old and looked in good need of a new lick of paint. Hugo noticed Mrs Seymour give it a few pained glances. They went around the side to the backyard and came upon the farmer just as he was emerging from the cowshed.

"Mr Kent," Mrs Seymour called, and he turned to squint at his landlady, wiping his hands on his breeches. "How do you do?"

"How do you do," repeated the farmer, in a low, mocking voice, and he gave a little bow. "Ma'am." Hugh, drawing up a few paces behind Mrs Seymour, was surprised by the open hostility in Kent's stare; the man had seemed perfectly amiable when he had met him a few hours before.

"I am very well, thank you, Kent." Mrs Seymour folded her hands before her and seemed, for a moment, to be searching for the right words. "I thought I'd better come and tell you that your little boy Robbie has been caught killing a hare in the wood. Now, since it hasn't happened before, of course we won't be too severe on him..."

"No, I reckon not," muttered Kent, turning his gaze away from her for a moment and toward the backdoor of his house, which was hanging a little off its hinges. "Only haul him before the magistrate and have him locked away, I suppose."

"No, no! There is no question of that, Kent. I want to assure you—"

"And what's your assurance worth, ma'am?" The farmer looked back at her. He was flushed in the face now and breathing hard. "Let me ask you that. Why should I believe a word any of you people say?"

Mrs Seymour stood absolutely still. But her voice, when she spoke a moment later, was not haughty or offended; she sounded almost gentle. Hugh's surprise was increasing by the second. "I know you are angry. I know that you have come to expect the worst from us." She held up her hands, as if in supplication or surrender. "My housekeeper Simms is looking after Robbie at the moment, and I will send him home to you this evening. All I ask is that you reprimand him and make him see why he can't do such a thing again."

"Aye, I can give you that assurance," said the farmer. He deliberated for a moment, and then, pointedly, "And what's more, I'll stick to it, too." He spat on the ground.

Hugh could take no more of this: he sprang forward. "Sir, you will apologise to the lady at once—"

"Jorkins, please." Mrs Seymour laid a gloved hand on his arm, stopping him before he could get any further. The farmer was already turning away from them, moving toward his backdoor. Hugh saw a pale face peering out at them from the window. He shook his head, turning back to Mrs Seymour.

"He ought to show you more respect," he said.

"Why should he?" she said, quietly. "Respect must be earned, and we have done nothing to earn it from them."

"You could have punished their boy more severely, but you didn't!" Hugh pointed out, following after her as she started back toward the carriage.

"Because that family has been punished enough."

"What—" But Hugh got no further, for reaching the farmyard gate, he looked down and saw the tears on Mrs Seymour's cheeks. He blinked in surprise and reached in his pocket to hand her a clean handkerchief.

She thanked him and dabbed at her eyes before pressing on to the carriage. Hugh handed her in, her small, gloved hand in his rough bare one, and Mrs Seymour said, once she had sat, "You never met my husband, Mr Jorkins. If you had known him when he was alive, I daresay you would understand."

With that, the carriage door closed, and Hugh Jorkins, after his first meeting with Mrs Seymour, was left with the sense that he was missing a part of a much larger puzzle.

~

Ivy Kent was not at home when Mr Jorkins and Mrs Seymour called upon her father. She was the eldest girl in the family, and at sixteen, was out looking for work in town. She was not quite pretty: she was sturdy-limbed, with a bold green stare and freckles on her nose, and always wore her dark hair scraped back in a bun. Her figure was well-known on Main Street, and there were two reasons for this: the first was that she had skivvied for a number of families in Hartleton when she was younger, and the second was that it was rumoured she was Mr John Seymour's natural daughter.

The rumour was never spoken of in her own household. Ivy had grown up hearing the whispers from classmates and neighbours, but her own parents had never alluded to it in her presence, only looked at her sometimes a little sadly or a little strangely. She knew that Mr Seymour had never acknowledged the connection; had never sent her mother any compensation; had neglected them and his other tenants, even as their farm fell into disrepair and their winters became harsh and hungry. Now that he was dead, his widow seemed to be trying to make amends, but none of the Kents trusted her, either. She had known, after all, about her husband, hadn't she? Wasn't it her fault, wasn't there something lacking in her that had caused him to stray so frequently and so disastrously?

At any rate, Ivy was a familiar figure in Hartleton, and she received a few nods and smiles as she passed down the street. She was just passing Mr White's warehouse when someone grabbed her around the waist.

"Watch it!" she exclaimed, and then erupted into giggles as she craned her neck around and saw who was holding her. "Oh, Cecil, you are bad!"

"Did I scare you?" said Cecil Simms, pressing kisses all over her face, which she had eagerly offered up to him. "I'm sorry. I couldn't help it, you looked so serious..."

"Well, I was thinking about something very important," Ivy said, affecting a tone of offended dignity, which was not helped by the fact that Cecil was still kissing her. "I was trying to work out how long I'd have to save for a new dress on three shillings a week."

Cecil wrinkled his brow and stuck out his lower lip a little, as though he were thinking. He pulled back from Ivy and drew her arm through his own as they started to walk. "Well, I suppose it depends on how nice the dress is."

"As long as it's nicer than this one," said Ivy, looking down at her faded pink print with distaste.

"Oh, but I think it's so pretty." Cecil bent and dropped a kiss behind her ear.

"Cecil, stop, people are looking." But Ivy's tone completely belied her words, as she threaded Cecil's arm closer through hers and leaned on him a little. "It isn't proper, you know."

"I'll be good, I promise."

"You've promised me things before." Ivy was smiling broadly. "You promised to be a gentleman that time, and you didn't keep your word, did you?"

"Ah, but there's a good reason for that." Cecil turned around, finding her hand and interlacing their fingers. Both of their hands were calloused and rough. "I just can't help myself when I'm with you. Because..." He lowered his voice to a stage whisper, almost mouthing, "Because I love you, Ivy Kent."

"You're silly," Ivy said, tugging them both along again. She was blushing furiously, and her heart was fluttering in her chest.

"Aren't you going to say you love me too?"

"I don't love you, I think you're very silly." As she spoke, Ivy turned her eyes back on Cecil. She was young and had not yet encountered any reason why she ought to guard her emotions; she could not possibly have known how much plain adoration showed in her face at that moment. She just looked at Cecil as she had always looked at him. He had always seemed a long way beyond her, not just because he was a few years older, but because he was so handsome and clever and important: the most handsome, clever, and important man in Hartleton, in Ivy's opinion, and it was sometimes difficult to believe that he had chosen her.

"You wound me," said Cecil, grandly. "You cut me to the core."

"All right, then maybe I love you a little bit. Sometimes. Will you walk to Mrs Gordon's with me? I have an interview."

"That's at the other side of town," Cecil grumbled. "You know I've already walked all the way from Highfield."

"Well, I didn't ask you to, did I?"

"You really are cruel. I've half a mind to leave you to fend for yourself." Cecil stopped them both outside the post office, and Ivy raised her eyes to his face, half-fearful that he meant his words. But he just swung her hand back and forth a little and then said, casually, "You know, I know someone much closer who's looking for a maid."

"Who?"

"Mr Jorkins."

"Mr Jorkins?" Ivy frowned. "Isn't he staying in your aunt's boarding house?"

"He's just taken rooms upstairs from Johnson's," said Cecil, pointing across the street to the haberdasher's. "And he needs one maid, to clean for him and cook his meals."

"How do you know all this?"

Cecil shrugged his shoulders. "Aunt Maggie told me. She said she'd help him find someone. Well, are you interested or not?"

"How much will he pay a week?"

"I don't know, two, three shillings..." As Ivy frowned, considering, Cecil added, impatiently, "Oh, don't bother doing the sums now. Come on, let's go talk to my aunt." He put a hand on the small of her back and steered her on toward the boarding house.

It was a party of four ladies that set out from Highfield House that afternoon. They barely fit into the carriage; the generous frames of Mrs White and Mrs Aldridge, enhanced by their crinolines, took up a good deal of space. Demelza found her elbow constantly jostled by Gertrude during the drive, as the other young lady pointed out things and people of interest. Farmers, manufacturers and curates were named to Demelza, and in each case, Gertrude was able to list whom they had married, whether they came from Hartleton or from further afield, and in what particular church they might (or might not) be spotted on a Sunday. It was clear that she made the parish of Hartleton her study.

When they were driving through the entrance to the estate, Demelza, looking out the carriage window, had one of those strange transports of memory that break down the barrier of years, as she saw the canopy of trees settle into place overhead. For a moment, she was sure that it was her mother at her elbow rather than Gertrude. And then the carriage jolted as it ran over a pothole, and Mrs Aldridge made some remark about the bad quality of the drive, and just like that, she was back in the present.

"It is a shame that they don't keep the place better," Mrs White agreed with her sister. Then, with a pointed look at Gertrude, "But you, of course, my dear, will remedy that in good time."

Demelza glanced at her step-cousin, expecting her to be pleased, and was surprised to see that Gertrude coloured angrily. "Really, Mother, you mustn't talk so."

"But—my dear..."

"And why mustn't she?" demanded Mrs Aldridge. "You're a pretty young girl, and Nate Seymour is a charming young man, and when you are married, you'll manage that estate much better than his mother. Really, these things are not so very complicated, Gertrude."

"But it isn't proper," Gertrude continued to protest, and she really seemed distressed. Catching Demelza's sympathetic glance, she added, with renewed confidence, "And it isn't decided, not yet. What will Demi think of us, talking like this?"

"What does it matter what she thinks?" Mrs Aldridge exclaimed, and she really looked genuinely flummoxed. "You mustn't be so modest, Gertrude. Josephine, tell her."

"Last April in London," added Mrs White, eagerly, "Mrs Campbell overheard Nathaniel Seymour say that he liked you better than any other young lady he had danced with."

"That may be, Mother," said Gertrude, "But until he has made me an offer, we ought not to talk so freely about it."

"The girl is right, of course, Josephine." Mrs Aldridge shifted in her seat as the carriage came to a halt. "We must let the young people move at their own pace."

Mrs White made a sound of reluctant assent, and as they proceeded out of the carriage one by one, Gertrude took hold of Demelza's arm. "Please tell me honestly," she said quietly. "Once you have seen us together. Tell me what you think."

Demelza could only nod. She felt simultaneously moved and annoyed by the appeal. And despite her sad realisation of the night before, namely, that Nathaniel Seymour stood much larger in her memory than she probably did in his own, faint at the back of her mind was the possibility that things might not be as Gertrude, or Mrs White, or Mrs Aldridge all thought; that Nathaniel Seymour's feelings might not be so straightforward, that perhaps he might remember Demelza when he saw her, and like her better than Gertrude. What would she tell her cousin then? Would she be honest?

She need not have worried. Upon their entry into Hazelhurst Grange, it all became quite clear. They were walked through the hall, where their footsteps rang out with a great echo, and where footmen were posted on ladders polishing the chandelier for the upcoming ball. The three Seymours received them in the drawing room, and in the confusion of bowing and shaking hands, Demelza could see one thing: Gertrude was a favourite. His mother liked her, his sister liked her, he liked her.

Nathaniel was not very changed from when Demelza had last seen him. At fourteen he had been a tall young fellow, and at twenty he was simply taller and leaner. His red curls had darkened to auburn, but he still had the same ready smile, and those same pale blue eyes passed right through Demelza once introductions had been made, to return to Gertrude.

And it was strange, because Demelza remembered wishing that she belonged in such a pretty drawing-room. How many times had she sneaked up there as a child, to hide behind the curtains and pretend she was a part of it all? Yet that afternoon, she could think of nothing worse than sitting there, quietly sweating into her black stuff dress, while talk flowed back and forth around her of places and names of which she knew nothing. And all the while, her rebellious gaze kept drifting towards Nathaniel—Mr Seymour, she kept correcting herself, but her mind was rebellious, too—and she began to think longingly of open skies and fresh air, as though she had been perched on the edge of that ottoman for much longer than a half-hour.

Once their party had broken into smaller groups, things became a little more bearable, and an opportunity to escape presented itself. Nathaniel and Gertrude withdrew to the other side of the room with Letitia to look at her drawings, Mrs Seymour and Mrs Aldridge began talking about girls' schools, and Mrs White rose from her seat with a creak of skirts and declared that she was going to go downstairs to get a recipe from the cook.

"May I come?" said Demelza, at once.

"And why should you want to go downstairs?" Mrs White's voice was so loud that even the trio at the other end of the room glanced around from the drawing. Demelza winced.

"I know the housekeeper, Mrs Simms." She kept her own voice down, as Mrs White continued to stare at her suspiciously. Then, a flash of inspiration struck. "I was very troublesome to her when I was younger, and I think I'd better apologise."

"Hmph." Mrs White had been put in a difficult position, as to disagree with Demelza would have been to say that she was not troublesome. "Very well, then, come along."

Nathaniel sometimes felt that his mother saw him as a kind of delicate flower, someone to be protected rather than someone she could lean on, someone who might wither if exposed to the elements for too long. This uncomfortable feeling of his had been confirmed that morning, when she called upon their tenants without telling him, and came back with puffy eyes.

"It's my responsibility, Mother, and not yours," he argued with her as soon as they were out of the earshot of the servants. "All of these repairs and improvements are things that Father should have undertaken years ago. But he didn't, and now it falls to me."

"Not yet," Clara Seymour said neutrally. "And I thought it would be wiser to deal with the Kent boy myself."

"The Kent boy?"

"Yes, dear, the one who was caught poaching in the wood."

Nathaniel breathed in deeply through his nose. "You see? This is precisely what I am talking about. Letty, tell her." But his sister was looking out the window of the breakfast room, and not attending to their conversation. "I need to know these things, Mother. I need to know what is going on in my own estate. Would you prefer that I come into it fully unprepared for the responsibility?"

"I would prefer to spare you the hatred of those your father wronged for a little longer." His mother put down her embroidery, and he heard the emotion trembling under her voice. "Just until you are of age and married. Then you will be able to shoulder it."

Nathaniel shut his eyes for a moment, considering his mother's words. "If you are talking of the Kents, then I don't deny that they have been wronged. But it does not follow that you must take that burden on yourself."

"Why not? Is that not what a wife agrees, when she marries? To take on her husband's burdens as her own?"

"I wouldn't know," said Nathaniel, after a moment's pause, with the consciousness that he had been beaten: once older people began to talk in that way, there was nothing he could really add.

Then Letty, from her faithful post, announced that a carriage had just come up, and they went through to the drawing room to greet their guests. Things got much worse from there. If Nathaniel's mother saw him as a delicate flower, Mrs White and Mrs Aldridge were even worse; under their avid gazes, he felt as though he had been stripped down and placed under a bright light. Every small movement he made was exciting to them, every word he uttered seemed to tap deeper into a well of delight. He had the strange sense that if the butler had set up a turnstile outside the drawing room and placed him in an exhibit, these ladies would have happily bought tickets and contented themselves with peering at him through the glass.

Gertrude wasn't as irritating in her admiration of him, although that might have something to do with the fact that she was young and pretty; Nathaniel was not immune to such considerations. He was relieved, in any case, when his sister rescued him from Mrs White's endless round of questions and dragged him and Gertrude over to look at her drawings.

They had been thumbing through her sketchbook for a few minutes when Gertrude said, "Where is Demi?"

Nathaniel and Letty looked at one another in some confusion; his sister, grasping before he did that Gertrude was referring to the pale, silent companion in their party, said, "You mean Miss Abbott?"

"Yes, I call her Demi for short. She's very sweet. I thought she had come with us," Gertrude concluded, a little vaguely. She glanced around the drawing room before returning to her admiration of Letty's drawings. "But how you have played with the light and shade in this one, Miss Seymour! I do admire you."

Nathaniel was frowning, trying to work out in his head why Miss Abbott's name sounded so familiar, when he saw the butler enter and go to speak to his mother. In a flash, he was at her side. "What is it?"

Mrs Seymour dismissed the butler and turned to her son reluctantly. "It is the Kent boy," she said in a low voice. "We were supposed to keep him here until evening, you know, to reprimand him. But he has disappeared."

"I will go," said Nathaniel, simply, and held his mother's gaze for a long moment before she bent her head and assented. As he walked away, he heard Mrs Aldridge murmur in reverent tones, "Such a dutiful son," and felt like grinding his teeth.

It was not difficult to guess where a rebellious boy might have run to. From the kitchen door was a broad stretch of lawn leading straight to the wood, and though Demelza had been terrified of the trees herself as a child, she knew better than to attribute that fear to a boy who had probably grown up surrounded by them.

So once again, she felt the canopy of trees close in above her head, and once again, she felt the last few years drain away as though they had been nothing. There was no sound but the crackle of twigs under her feet. The air was wet and fresh in her lungs. Demelza felt the lack of her bonnet; a few strands of hair had already come loose from the loops behind her ears. But she had not been planning on going outside; she had only intended to drop in on Mrs Simms, and, upon finding the housekeeper in distress because of the missing boy, had ended up joining the search instead.

Every now and then, she heard the distant shout of one of the other servants who had come to look for Robbie Kent. But Demelza's feet were sure; she had walked this way so many times, after all. She was surprised to find what a short walk it was, the walk that had seemed so long to her childish mind. A layer of pine needles and mulch lay on the steps leading up to the cabin, and ivy was growing over the roof. A spiderweb of cracks spread through the glass of one of the windows.

"Robbie?" Demelza said, her boots crunching as she came up the steps. She knocked on the door, which stood slightly ajar, and said after a moment into the silence, "I know you're in there."

Silence stretched on a moment longer, and then she heard a sigh, and a boy emerged from behind the door. He looked about ten, with a scowling face and hair sticking up in all directions. "How d'you know?"

"It's a good hiding place."

"Who are you?" He looked her up and down. "You look like one of those funny Quaker ladies."

She laughed. It felt good to laugh. "I'm Demelza. I used to live here, you know."

"Here?" He cast a distasteful glance back at the cabin, and Demelza nodded. Robbie looked disappointed. "So you're poor then."

"Yes, I'm afraid so."

"My family's poor, too." Robbie went to lean against the railing, with his hands in his pockets like a little man. "It's why I set a trap for that hare." He cast her another dubious glance. "I suppose you know all about that."

"I know that you're supposed to be serving your punishment back in the house." Demelza spread out her shawl on the step and sat, crossing her legs and propping her elbows on her lap. "How bad was it? Did Mrs Simms have you folding napkins or licking envelopes?"

"I just don't like it there," Robbie said curtly. "I'm not going back. Go find my sister and tell her to get me here."

"Where's your sister?" said Demelza, who hadn't moved.

"Oh... I don't know." He sounded annoyed that she was questioning his logic. "Never mind. I don't want to go home anyway, either. Dad'll give me a lashing."

"Then where will you go?"

"I don't know. Maybe I'll just live here. Catch my own food. Make a campfire. Hide in the trees whenever anyone tries to find me."

Demelza kicked a dead leaf with her foot and said thoughtfully, "That doesn't sound so bad. Can I live here, too?"

"You're funny," said Robbie, but he came and sat on the step beside her. They heard someone shout, somewhere nearby in the trees, and then a dog's bark. Demelza started.

"What?" said Robbie, scornfully. "You're not scared of dogs, are you?"

"I am," Demelza admitted. "I used to live in this horrid school. And the woman who owned it—she's horrid, too— she owned this awful pitbull who would sleep at the bottom of the stairs, to stop the girls from running away."

"Did you ever try to run away?"

"Oh, yes, more than once."

"Did the dog ever bite you?"

"Yes, on the leg."

"Did it hurt? Do you have a scar? Can I see?"

"That wouldn't be proper," said Demelza, smiling. Robbie seemed impressed anyway. He gave a low whistle, and then glanced around as another bark sounded, closer by.

"Are you going back to hide?" she asked him, rising from her seat and brushing herself down. "I won't give you away. Though I'd prefer not to walk back on my own."

Robbie sighed and got up. "Dogs are nice. You'll see." But he put his hand in Demelza's, and asked as they started walking, "So are you going to be an old maid, then?"

Nathaniel Seymour met them a little way down the path, accompanied by another servant. It was his pointer that had been barking, and the dog jumped for Robbie, who laughed and fell to petting and stroking his fur.

"See?" Robbie said to Demelza, who had automatically backed away a step. "He's not so bad, is he?"

"I suppose he isn't," she said, hesitantly.

"Well, don't just suppose—pet him."

Nathaniel cleared his throat. "Robbie?"

"Yes, sir?" The boy straightened, and gently pushed the pointer back, who was still trying to leap up to lick his face. "Down. Get down, will you." Demelza felt a wild, nervous laugh building in her throat.

"Here, Jack," said Nathaniel, sharply, and the dog returned to his side meekly. "Robbie, are you sorry for running away? You gave everyone a lot of trouble, you know."

"Yes, sir. I'm sorry, sir." Robbie lowered his eyes. Demelza squeezed his hand in reassurance.

"Mrs Simms has some more work for you, I daresay. Will you go back and help her, and show you're sorry for killing that hare?"

"Yes, sir."

"Carling, take him back." Nathaniel shifted out of the way to let the boy pass. Robbie dropped Demelza's hand, mouthed something at her and pointed at the dog before departing. She smiled.

"Thank you for finding him, Miss Abbott."

"Oh, it was nothing, I—"

"Your party has been worried about you too. We had better get back." Nathaniel turned on his heel and walked on, all stiff formality. Demelza stared at his uncompromising back for a moment before following on behind him.

Afternoon had lengthened into evening, and summer shadows drifted along the grass as they emerged from the trees. Her eyes on the forbidding facade of the house that loomed ahead, Demelza hung back a little. Nathaniel's dog had gone rooting in the brush, and she clicked her tongue and then called, "Jack? Jack!"

"Leave him," Nathaniel said over his shoulder, but his dog had already come shooting back, nearly bowling Demelza over. She caught her balance, steadying her hand on the dog's head, and started to laugh.

Nathaniel Seymour turned around. In the strange half-light between afternoon and evening, his eyes were all the bluer. Demelza was stooped down, scratching Jack's ears, and fresh in her delight, she met Nathaniel's gaze.

In the carriage on the way back to Highfield House, when Mrs Aldridge and Mrs White had taken a break from scolding Demelza for getting mud on her shawl and petticoat, Gertrude said in her ear, "What do you think?"

Demelza, whose excursion from the woods had left her a little tired and flat, an uncomfortable reminder that not so long ago she had been too weak to get out of bed, turned to face her step-cousin. "I think he does like you," she said quietly, and sincerely. "Very much."

Like all such moments, after all, the one between her and Nathaniel had passed away quickly. She had seen the smile fade from his lips, and his eyes drop away from her own. She had seen the way those same eyes followed Gertrude when they said their goodbyes. These things were straightforward enough in the end, as Mrs Aldridge had said.

Ivy Kent knew that nothing in life ever came easily, at least not for people like her. So it wasn't really surprising when Cecil informed her of the condition that would come with her working for Mr Jorkins.

She was happy enough to do it, too. Mr Jorkins seemed nice enough, but it was evident that he wasn't of her sort. It seemed that Hugh Jorkins was trying to ingratiate himself with the Seymours. That was what she had pieced together, in any case, from what Cecil and her father told her. As well as that, the rooms above the haberdasher's were closer to the farm than any other post in town she could have gotten, and she wasn't about to go passing that up because of a few scruples.

It was on the evening of her second day working for Mr Jorkins that Ivy came into his study to find him writing a letter. From the windows that faced onto the street, the lights of the town cast a faint glow upon his desk. The only other source of illumination was a candle burning close to his elbow.

"Sir?" she said, folding her hands in front of her apron, and he started up and nearly upended his bottle of ink.

"Oh—Ivy. I'm sorry, I'm still not used to having someone else around." He half-turned in his seat, with a gentle smile. He was a good-looking man, Ivy thought. She could see by the greying stubble on his chin that he had forgotten to shave this morning. His eyes looked bloodshot and tired, and he was in his shirtsleeves. And then, before her scruples could develop beyond a few uneasy stirrings, she quickly said,

"Will you be needing anything else, sir? I've swept up the hall and stocked up the fire."

"Oh..." He considered for a moment, tapping his ink-stained fingers on the desk. "No, thank you, Ivy. You may go home for the evening."

"You're sure, sir?" Ivy's eyes had caught on the letter, and she took a step forward to see if she could make out the address, but at the same moment, Mr Jorkins's restless fingers came down to block it from sight. "You wouldn't—like a cup of tea, or anything?"

"No, thank you, Ivy. Goodnight."

"You didn't offer to post the letter?" Cecil exclaimed, a half-hour later. He was leaning against a doorframe in the warehouse. It was deserted at this hour of the evening, and the streets of Hartleton were quiet, too.

"No post goes this late," said Ivy, feebly.

"You could've made something up! Then you could've seen who it was for."

"Well, I didn't think of that, did I." She folded her arms and looked off in the other direction. "I'm sorry I'm not as clever as you. But, you know, when I went looking for work I wasn't exactly planning on being a spy..."

"Don't say 'spy'." Cecil took hold of her hands, forcing her to look back at him. "Don't use that word. All right, Ivy? You're just keeping a lookout for any strange behaviour."

"Well, I haven't seen any strange behaviour," she grumbled. "Unless you call posting a letter strange behaviour..."

"Ssh, will you." Cecil cast a nervous glance at the chink of light under the door to Mr White's office. "Look, wait for me outside. I'll be out in a few minutes."

Mr White had long since gone home, and it was James Quigley who was currently occupying his office. The lawyer looked up from his papers as Cecil entered. "Well, well. Learned anything useful?"

"No, sir," Cecil said, without meeting his master's gaze. "Ivy saw Mr Jorkins writing a letter, but she didn't see the address."

"Ah, a pity. Well, Cecil..." Mr Quigley stretched back in his seat, rolling his stiff shoulders. "Is it not your night off? You ought to go home and rest. You've done a good day's work."

"Yes, sir. Thank you, sir." Cecil bowed, but he felt far from satisfied. He had not done a good day's work, and he could feel the restlessness tingling all over him. Of course, it was not all his fault: the incompetence of certain other people had played a role, too. But he was not the housekeeper's boy anymore; he was a valet, a gentleman's gentleman. So he got as far as the door, and finally paused. "Sir?"

"Yes, Cecil?"

Cecil turned, and summoned all the calm that he could as he met his master's gaze. "You know that you can rely on me, sir. Anything that you wish to have carried out, I will do it. And I will not ask questions."

"Thank you, Cecil." Mr Quigley sounded amused; Cecil felt a flush spread in his cheeks. "But what I want is really not so very complicated or underhanded. I simply want Hartleton to be free of the presence of Mr Jorkins. I believe that he is a dangerous man."

Cecil inclined his head in acknowledgement of this. "But it seems, sir, that he will not be leaving any time soon. Ivy said that he visited her parents' farm yesterday with Mrs Seymour. He seems to take his business very seriously."

"It is not business that brings him here," Mr Quigley said, scornfully. "At least, not business of the kind you are thinking." He pushed back his chair and stood, pulling out a valise. But rather than elaborating on this tantalising tidbit, he said instead, "Let me ask you something, Cecil. Have you and Ivy known one another for a long time?"

"Since we were children, sir."

"Indeed. And..." Sweeping his papers into the valise, Mr Quigley added, "How far would she be willing to go for you, do you think, Cecil?"

"Well—" Cecil hesitated only for a moment. "She loves me, sir. I think she would do anything."

"You think?" Mr Quigley's eyes were cold and assessing behind his spectacles.

"I know." Having corrected himself, Cecil quickly went on, with a new surge of confidence, "I promise that I can manage her, sir."

"Well, then." Mr Quigley passed him out, moving for the door. "We will make sure that Hugh Jorkins does not menace Hartleton anymore."

~

On Sunday, church bells rang out across the valley, and townspeople peered at one another in their pews rather than listening to the minister. Nathaniel left in the middle of the closing hymn, ignoring the curious glances of his mother and sister.

Outside, a strong wind was blowing, and there was a smell of salt on the air, though the sea was miles away. Nathaniel bowed his head under it as he entered the graveyard, tucking his cravat under the lapels of his coat. It did not take him long to reach his father's grave, and he stood in front of it for some time without looking at the inscription.

Down here, there was a view of hills all around. Behind one hill was the London road, behind another, the wood that surrounded Hazelhurst Grange. Nathaniel's eyes passed between these, and then, catching a movement in the periphery of his vision, he turned to see a figure in black nearby. She knelt to lay flowers before a modest headstone, and then straightened, and as the wind tugged out blonde strands from her black bonnet, Nathaniel knew that it was her.

Six years ago, she had been a fairy child, fresh and enchanting. And now she was already beaten down, tired with life. She was pale with shadows under her eyes. Seeing her with Robbie Kent the other day had brought it home to Nathaniel, the fact that those two were just the same. Here was yet another person that his father's greed and hunger had brought low. How would Nathaniel ever even begin to make amends?

Demelza stopped on her way out of the graveyard, bobbing a curtsey in his direction. He bowed in response and hoped she would not speak. When her name was called by one of her step-aunts standing at the gate, drifting on the air towards them, Nathaniel breathed a sigh of relief as he watched her go.

4

MAIDS AND LADIES

Demelza felt that a weight had lifted from her shoulders when, at the end of her first week in Hartleton, Mrs Aldridge left to return to Bristol. What she had not reckoned with was the tyranny of Mrs White, whom she had always cast in her mind as the more passive of the two; their only difference, Demelza was soon to find, lay in how they dispatched their orders. When Mrs Aldridge wanted something done, she gave the order and was obeyed; Mrs White, by contrast, seemed to feel the need to soften the order by suggesting the inherent good it would do to Demelza, and this, by far, was the more offensive approach.

So Demelza, after rising early to write letters to various households that had advertised for a governess, was interrupted in her task by Mrs White. Her step-aunt entered the gable-room, looked out at the thick fog shrouding the valley and said that it would be a good thing for Demelza to get some exercise, and, while she was it, to pick up some orders from the greengrocer and the butcher. They were to entertain that evening; the Seymours were returning their visit by dining at Highfield House, and so, of course, there were many necessaries to be purchased.

The nature of Demelza's illness had been such that it made her particularly vulnerable to the damp in the air. She made slow progress on her walk, and took frequent rests by leaning against a stile or sitting on an upturned stone. By the time she got into town, the fog had cleared, which was some relief to her, and she stepped into the post office first to send off the letters she had written.

There was a gentleman at the counter who had come before her. Demelza, still out of breath, only saw the back of his head, and she was not attending when he turned around. It was all the more of a shock to her, therefore, when he stopped before her and extended a hand.

"My God! Are you Demelza?"

She gave a start. The gentleman had flecks of grey in his dark hair, and his face was tanned and weatherbeaten, but there was an energy and youthfulness to his movements that suggested he was younger than forty. Demelza could not conceive of how she could possibly know him, when the gentleman added, "You look just like your father. I met him, you know, before he and Esther married."

"Uncle Hugh!" she exclaimed then and was rewarded by a kind smile.

"So you do recognise me. I wanted to test you. Esther showed you a picture of me, I suppose? For we look nothing alike, as a brother and sister go."

"Y-yes," Demelza lied. Her mother had never shown her any picture of Hugh, but she was not about to mention that she had heard her relatives discussing his arrival in ominous tones. "You are—you are staying in Hartleton?"

"For the time being." A strange quality entered her uncle's tone, and he half-turned his head toward the post-mistress, who was listening intently to their conversation. "Forgive me, Demelza, did you have to post a letter? I shall wait for you outside."

Demelza hurriedly carried out her business, in so great a confusion that the post-mistress had to ask her the same question three times, and came out to find Mr Jorkins waiting for her, as he had promised. They proceeded a little way down main street, maintaining an awkward distance between them.

"I have tried calling at Highfield House," her uncle said, breaking the silence. "I was anxious to see you. But the servant always turns me away."

"Cecil, I suppose?" Demelza said, with some distaste. "He's my stepfather's valet. He's... rather unpleasant."

"Not just him. The maid, too. It seems..." Mr Jorkins paused. "It seems whenever I call, that no one is at home." He glanced at Demelza. "But that cannot be, surely?"

"Well—I don't know." What was she supposed to say? She'd had no idea that he was calling at the house; all she knew was that her relatives seemed to dislike him, and this wasn't something she could say outright; however, he went on, a moment later,

"I'm afraid that Mr Quigley and I have crossed paths a few times since your mother's funeral, and found that we didn't see eye to eye. Perhaps, as your guardian, he sees fit to keep me away."

Demelza bowed her head. Her uncle continued, watching her profile, "I do not mean to cast aspersions on Mr Quigley; but let me just tell you, Demelza, that you are not alone. I know that I have been away for years, but I am here now, though the circumstances are sadder than I would have liked..."

"Thank you, uncle," she said, sensing by a sudden dip of his tone that he was going to introduce her mother, and wanting to steer away from that dangerous topic. He had been to the funeral and she had not; he had the claim of many years over her in knowing her mother, and it was something she could not think about at that moment. Who knew what she might say, when that wave of grief rose again to claim her? "I hope you will come to dinner at Highfield House soon."

"Yes, I do too," said her uncle, rather pointedly, and Demelza made her excuses. When they had parted ways, she turned her thoughts to the list Mrs White had given her, fearing that if she let them dwell on Mr Jorkins for too long, she might burst into tears at any moment.

Nathaniel, having won a victory over his mother after the affair with the Kent boy (although he really owed that victory to Demelza fetching him, but he wasn't going to think about that), went about pursuing the business of the estate with a new confidence, and he was about to set out to supervise repairs on the outer walls when a hired carriage rolled up the drive, and out hopped a young gentleman, fashionably dressed, with brown hair to his shoulders and a wicked smile.

"Frank!" Nathaniel exclaimed, putting away his gloves and going forward to meet his friend. "Well, well, what a surprise!"

"Not an unpleasant one, I hope," grinned Frank. "I know I said I'd come on Friday. But, well, there wasn't much going on in town, and I thought I might look around here and make a study of provincial life. Is the shooting here any good?"

"Well—it's..." Nathaniel, a little overwhelmed by all the questions, shook his head as though to clear it. "Come in, and we'll talk properly."

"Oh, I'm sorry, old boy," said Frank, following him into the hall and letting the butler take his coat. "Were you just about to go out?"

"No, no," said Nathaniel, who was polite to a fault, even as he felt his heart sink at the sight of his mother coming out to greet them. "Mother, this is the friend from Oxford whom I told you about, Frank Honeychurch."

"Delighted to make your acquaintance, Mrs Seymour," said Frank, with a deep bow and a charming smile. "Though I must confess, I thought for a moment that I was meeting Nate's sister."

"How very kind," said Mrs Seymour, with a wry smile.

"Apologies for the short notice. As I was telling Nate..." Frank gestured with his hat toward his friend, "I was supposed to be studying in town, but the charms of the countryside simply beckoned me from my books. So I took the new railway this morning and here I am before you."

"The railway!" repeated Nathaniel's mother. "How very interesting. I'm sure Nathaniel will want to hear all about that. And, you are earlier than expected, Mr Honeychurch, but I'm sure we are very glad to have you. We shall see about having the blue room made up—Mrs Simms?"

"Mother," Nathaniel began, in an undertone, foreseeing her interference, but she was running on,

"And I can go to meet Parsons now, Nathaniel; I am very happy to step in while you see that your guest is comfortably settled."

"Thank you, Mother," said Nathaniel stiffly, after a short pause, and Frank smiled between them.

"How splendid! Well, well, lead the way."

And his friend chattered on eagerly for the next half-hour as he was given the grand tour around the house, blissfully unaware that he had secured Mrs Seymour a victory, and set Nathaniel right back where he had started.

Clara Seymour was not ready to surrender the duties of the estate just because her son had finally decided to shoulder them, and she told herself that she was being perfectly reasonable. After all, what about all the time he had been absent? And what about all the time his father had been absent, even back when he was still alive? Over all the changes that had been wrought over Hazelhurst in the last few years, Clara had been the one constant, and she was not about to retreat to the drawing room again.

No, she had been shut up long enough; her spirit was one that longed for fresh air and freedom. As well as that—and Clara would not have admitted this to anyone, least of all to herself—there was the matter of Hugh Jorkins. He was a bit of a puzzle to her. He spoke like a gentleman, but had taken a role under Parsons, whose father was a farmer. The first time they had met, he had looked at her with such contempt, and yet stepped in to defend her against Mr Kent.

So she put on a greatcoat and heavy boots and set out through the wood, making for the stone wall that bordered the estate. There were several spots that had been worn down, some by the effects of time, others by mischief.

"Mrs Seymour," said Mr Jorkins, when she arrived at the designated spot, a part of the wall where, due to a depression in the ground, the wall did not quite reach it. He had been in conversation with Parsons but turned around and took off his hat to greet her. He looked a little surprised that she was more practically dressed today. "I was expecting your son."

"A friend of Nathaniel's just arrived from town," Clara explained, with a smile. "I thought it best that I take his place."

Mr Jorkins nodded, and they turned their attention to Parsons, who began to explain the labour that would be required to fill in this first gap in the wall. He concluded, "So you see, ma'am, it is not so very great. But if you will follow me this way, I will show you a spot further down that gives me more alarm; it is right by the wood path, and all but an invitation to poachers."

Hugh Jorkins fell into step with Clara as they followed Parsons. The path along the wall ran parallel to the wood, and the wind drifted through the trees toward them. Mr Jorkins pushed the dark hair off his brow, and Clara glanced at him. "You are quiet today, Jorkins."

"What—oh, yes. My apologies, ma'am."

"Is there something on your mind?"

"No, no," he said, and then, feeling that her gaze was still on him, he turned to look at her. There was something like a question in his eyes. Clara quickly looked away, but she wondered if her face had already given the answer.

"It is just—I am thinking about my niece," Jorkins said, after the awkward pause that followed.

"Miss Abbott?" Clara said, brightly, to cover up her confusion. "She came to visit here last week. She seems to have turned into a very... clever young lady." Although, when she actually thought about it, there was little else about Demelza Abbott that had stood out to her that day. She remembered one of those awful women, Mrs Aldridge or Mrs White, mentioning that the girl was destined to be a governess, and so 'clever' seemed as good a word as any. It was a pity, Clara reflected, how enchanting children often became quite dull when they were grown. At least, the same thing had not happened with her Nathaniel.

"I met her in town this morning," said Mr Jorkins, and Clara lost her train of thought. "For the first time since I arrived back in the country. She did not look altogether well. I am afraid that her stepfather and his sisters might be overworking her. She was ill, you know, at school."

"I did not know," Clara said quietly, thinking back to the girl's pale face. "And I am sorry for it."

"That was why she couldn't come to Esther's funeral. I am afraid—" Mr Jorkins stopped and shook his head. "I still must learn, I suppose, what it is to be an uncle."

Clara nodded her head, slowly. She did not trust herself to look at him now. Esther Quigley's name still sent a chill through her—there had been no mention of it when the Whites had called on the Grange last week—and it brought home, once more, the great chasm that lay between herself and Jorkins. She had known, of course, that he was Esther's sister, but they looked different enough that it had been possible to forget for a few moments. When she spoke again, it was in tones of undue formality. "Well, it is natural, after so long spent abroad. And I am sure that your niece is in good hands."

She passed on up the path, toward where Parsons had stopped by a crumbled section of the wall. Jorkins did not attempt to speak to her again that day.

～

Cecil Simms may have been Mr Quigley's valet, but there was a big difference between being a valet and being a common servant, and he didn't enjoy being treated as the latter. Such was the sad state of affairs on the evening when the Seymours were due to dine at Highfield House.

At half-past five, the kitchen was filled with smoke and other dubious odours; the maid was still on her knees scrubbing the stairs, and Cecil was pulled away from ironing his master's shirt to "help move the piano". Why it was necessary to move the piano, he had no idea. All he knew was that it weighed a ton, and he, Mr White and the boy who cleaned out the drains had to strain every muscle in their bodies to move it, while Mrs White stood in the doorway and gave unhelpful directions.

"To the left—no, no, my left...."

When at last the job was done, Cecil slipped away while the other two were still dusting off their hands and catching their breath. He plodded down the servants' stairs two steps at a time, and ducked through the kitchen.

"Where are you going?" thundered the cook. "You said you'd find someone to fix the oven door..."

"Master's orders," Cecil called back, and then he slammed the door behind him and stepped out into the narrow passage that ran between the kitchen gardens and the back of the house. From here, he could see lights winking on all over the valley, and it was all quite pretty, if you liked that kind of thing. He reached a long hand into his pocket and drew out a cigarette, lit it and inhaled deeply.

The sound of running footsteps disturbed his peace moments later, and he heard a familiar voice calling through the darkness, "Cecil! Cecil, where are you?"

"I'm here, but keep it down, will you," he hissed, throwing away his cigarette end as Ivy came around into the passage. "Where have you been? You said you'd come at four. We're up the walls here now."

"I couldn't get away before," Ivy said breathlessly; as Cecil's eyes adjusted to see her in darkness, he thought she looked as though she had run most of the way. "Mr Jorkins—he was working later than he thought and then he needed his supper..."

"Never mind, never mind." With a benevolent air, Cecil drew her in for a kiss. It lasted only for a moment, as the sound of a window opening above made them break apart hastily. Cecil pressed them back against the wall, peering up anxiously, but no one looked out, and he only heard Mrs White's voice giving orders to someone before it drifted away again.

"I'd better get back inside. Here." And he reached into his pocket again, drawing out a small packet in a brown paper bag, which he passed to Ivy. "Take good care no one sees you with it."

Her eyes were wide in the darkness, as she peeked inside. "What is it?"

"Doesn't matter," Cecil said swiftly. "Just do as we agreed." Then, as she continued to hesitate, he sighed and put his hands on her shoulders. "Go on, get going. I don't want you wandering around in the dark." He steered her along the passage. As they were passing the kitchen door, Ivy dug in her heels and turned back, forcing him to stop, too.

"What is it?" he said playfully. "Don't want to leave without a kiss goodbye, is that it?"

"Cecil." Ivy suddenly looked very young. She was not the sort to cry; she was too rough and steady for that, but he did see her lip tremble. "Cecil, I don't know about this."

"Remember what we said," he said patiently, as though coaxing her through her times tables. "Think of how it's going to help us."

"But Mr Jorkins isn't a—a bad man, he—" Ivy stopped dead as the door creaked open. All the colour drained from her face, and Cecil's lip curled as they saw Demelza standing in the doorway. She had her hair done up for dinner but was wearing an apron over her black dress.

"Cecil," she said, her gaze passing from Ivy's frightened face to his defiant one, "You'd better come in. The Seymours have arrived, and Cook's looking for you."

"Then we mustn't keep her waiting, I suppose," said Cecil blandly, and he gave Ivy's arm a hard squeeze before following Demelza inside.

At dinner, there was a fine variety of food and conversation. Demelza had been seated next to Mr Frank Honeychurch, the young man that the Seymours had brought with them, and she ate quietly as the others talked. Mr and Mrs White seemed to be trying to impress Mr Honeychurch with their refinement, and even Mr Quigley occasionally joined them in that endeavour. Meanwhile, Gertrude reserved all of her attentions for Nathaniel, and Mrs Seymour talked to her daughter.

Cecil came out with the maid to serve the soup, and as he moved around the table, his eyes inevitably met Demelza's over and over again. The candlelight reflected in his pupils made him look eerie, and every now and then, he would give a defiant tilt of the head, as though to remind her that she was a fool, and that she had not heard anything.

She was not so sure. The girl with him had looked upset, and the tremulous way she had said the name of Mr Jorkins had caught Demelza's attention as soon as she came to the door. Cecil's low tone, too, had left its imprint on her mind, as he said, *Think of how it's going to help us.* Why should they have been talking about her uncle? She thought of their meeting in town this morning, when he had tried to angle for an invitation to Highfield House and made her so uncomfortable. Did Mr Jorkins know something that she didn't?

After the main course had been served, the occupants of the table turned their attention to Mr Quigley, who began telling one of his rare anecdotes about how he had supported John Seymour when he had run as a Whig candidate a few years back. Mrs Seymour looked slightly pained, but everyone else seemed to be amused by the story. Demelza, who never could listen to her stepfather speak with much enjoyment, kept her gaze fixed on her plate, and was accordingly surprised when her neighbour addressed her.

"I hear, Miss Abbott, that you went to school in Bristol," said Mr Honeychurch, as he helped himself to the potato.

"Yes," she said, keenly aware that Mrs White had looked over from the other side of the table. "My Aunt Agnes owns an establishment there for young ladies."

"And is it a good establishment?"

"Yes," said Demelza again, stiffly. "I learned a great many things there." She glanced sidelong and caught a flash of white teeth as Mr Honeychurch smiled.

"But that is true of any school, is it not? Though often what we learn is not exactly what our teachers might have intended us to learn." He took a sip from his glass of wine and wiped his mouth delicately. "I am afraid I was a very poor student, Miss Abbott. Nate will tell you." Mr Honeychurch looked across the table to exchange a smile with his friend. Nathaniel's smile faded as he turned his attention back to Mr Quigley. "I still am a poor student."

"What do you study?"

"This year it is law." Frank Honeychurch shrugged. "Next year it might be the church. It seems I cannot settle to anything."

"I envy you," said Demelza, surprising herself with her own candour. Mr Honeychurch, however, simply raised his eyebrows and took another sip of wine. "I mean," she went on, quickly, "it seems wonderful to have so many talents that you are suited for a great number of different things."

"A wonder or a curse, depending on how you look at it."

Perhaps it was not so much what he said as the casual tone in which he said it that made something harden in Demelza. "I should think it a curse to be destined for one thing in your life, and to have no hope of any other," she said, coolly, and then Cecil came in again to clear their plates, and she only gave one-word answers to Mr Honeychurch's questions for the rest of dinner.

∾

After dinner, a game of whist was proposed. Gertrude, who was an avid card-player, glared at her father as he sat down opposite her and widened her eyes significantly in Nathaniel's direction, but it was too late; Nathaniel had already seated himself opposite Mr Quigley and joined his team. Closer to the fire, Mrs Seymour, Letty and Mrs White sat making stilted conversation, and Frank Honeychurch drew up a chair beside Demelza.

Nathaniel only let his eyes linger on that pair for a moment before looking back at Mr Quigley. He watched the lawyer as he dealt cards. "I was very interested by your story about my father at dinner."

"Oh, yes." Mr Quigley gave a small smile as he put down his last card. His dark eyes behind his glasses were enigmatic, and then on top there was the great shock of white hair that made him somewhat more distinguished than he had looked as a younger man, with curling fair hair. "Well, Mr Seymour, you know that I was very fond of your father. I am not sure now if he was made for politics, but he was certainly the kind of gentleman to try his best hand. Perhaps—" Dark eyes flicked upwards to regard Nathaniel. "Would you think of running, when you are of age?"

"No," said Nathaniel, with a little more vehemence than he had intended, and the other card-players glanced around at them.

"What are you talking of, James?" called Mrs White from across the room.

"We are talking of politics, dear Josephine," said Mr Quigley, raising his voice and tilting his chin up. When his sister responded with a sigh of disgust, he exchanged a conspiratorial smile with Nathaniel. "Well, that was my mistake, Mr Seymour. I ought to have sought an audience with you right after dinner. Politics is not a drawing-room conversation. But perhaps you might think on it a little."

"I—" Nathaniel was going to say that he did not need to think on it. Mr Quigley spoke to him just as his mother did, as though he was fresh out of the nursery, as though he might change his opinions at any given moment. But there was a severity to the lawyer's gaze which gave him pause. "I shall certainly have many things to think about, when I am of age."

"Yes indeed," replied Mr Quigley, mildly, and that was the end of that. Mrs Seymour, her daughter and Mrs White came over to watch the game, and Nathaniel, when it was not his turn, let his attention drift again. He looked to the fire, and saw Frank Honeychurch, leaning forward on his elbows as he talked to Demelza. He saw her in profile. She seemed earnest but utterly absorbed, in a way that he had not seen her before in company, and the heat of the fire had put some colour in her cheeks.

Mr Quigley won the trick, and Nathaniel told himself that this was the reason his mood had turned sour, as he gathered up his cards and dealt for the next round.

"I am afraid that I offended you at dinner," Mr Honeychurch said to Demelza, sitting down by her as the others began playing cards. "If you'll allow it, I shall explain myself: I am unaccustomed to thinking of anything besides my own comfort. The reality that others must work for a living, and often against their own wishes, is one that I don't consider enough."

Demelza put down her sewing and met Mr Honeychurch's gaze. She was on her last handkerchief now, a set of a dozen. And here was this fashionable young gentleman, with his flowing brown hair and easy smile, seeming quite earnest about wanting her approval. The reference to working for a living pained her: it reminded her of the letters that she had sent off this morning, of the fact that, quite soon, she might be taken away from Hartleton and from Nathaniel. Before her eyes could betray her by drifting in his direction, she made herself look back at Mr Honeychurch. "You need not apologise to me, sir. It was not my place to say such things as I did."

"But those things that you ought not to have said were very interesting," Mr Honeychurch argued, turning his chair more toward her, with a particular inflection in his tone that made her smile involuntarily. "What should you like to do, Miss Abbott?" He spread his hands. "Had you the command of the universe?"

"I should not like such a great responsibility." Demelza's smile was fully-formed now.

"But you would like to do something. Something other than what you are driven by necessity to do?"

His words touched something inside her; she could not help it. Demelza looked around to make sure that no one was listening before she said, "My father... when he was alive... owned his own industry. I visited his warehouse often when I was a child. I often thought... it would be fine, to make something new like that."

"Well." Frank Honeychurch leaned back in his chair, apparently satisfied. "There are many who would sniff at such an ambition, Miss Abbott. But I think it a fine one."

Demelza was not sure if he was in jest or in earnest; she looked up, about to reply, when Mrs White called to her brother, "What are you talking of, James?", her loud voice making them both jump. Frank and Demelza looked at one another, and with a sudden ease as though they were children, laughed.

"There is another way," Mr Honeychurch resumed, after the ladies sitting nearby had gone to look at the card game, giving them a bit more space to talk, "that I fear I might have offended you at dinner." His tone was more serious now. Demelza had resumed her work and listened to him comfortably. "My questions about your school might have seemed a little impertinent to you."

"It is not a thing I take great pleasure in discussing," she said, since he seemed to be waiting for her to say something.

"Because you were ill there?"

Demelza's eyes flashed up to Mr Honeychurch's, in confusion. He looked apologetic. "Mrs Seymour mentioned it."

"How did she..." Demelza looked over towards the card table, to find Mrs Seymour's eyes just flickering away, as though she had been watching her. "Yes, I was ill. Many of the girls were ill."

She was expecting further questions on Mr Honeychurch's part, and somewhat dreading them. Instead, he drew in a great breath, as though he were in some pain himself. "My sister went to such a school, a few years ago. Not in Bristol, but in Bath. But the ladies—and I hesitate to call them that— the ladies who ran it were negligent and cruel. There was an outbreak, and many of the girls fell ill, including herself. I thought I might lose her." Demelza, looking down, saw his closed fist trembling on his knee, as though in barely repressed anger.

"I am sure the suspense must have been very painful," she said gently. "I hope she is well now?"

"Oh! She is well. We got her out. But I'm sorry..." Frank Honeychurch hesitated, glancing around the room. "I'm sorry you do not have better friends."

Demelza almost thanked him from the bottom of her heart; she wanted to agree with him, to pour out all her troubles and sorrows—that something which his concern had touched within her was beginning to melt. But she checked herself just in time, holding herself apart. "They are my friends, all the same, Mr Honeychurch. And perhaps you should reserve your judgements until you get to know them better."

A light rain was falling when the Seymour party finally came out of Highfield House, and there was some scuffle as one of the servants tried to find an umbrella for Mrs Seymour. Standing by the carriage together, Frank said to Nathaniel, "Miss Abbott is a very serious girl."

"Is she?" said Nathaniel, affecting disinterest. He looked up at the house, and found his gaze momentarily drawn to a gable window. As he watched, a light struck up, as though by a match, and a small shadow moved against the curtains.

"Yes, she was very stern with me. But I rather think I deserved it. I was trying to get her opinion on everything and everyone, and I evidently took it too far."

"Everyone?" Nathaniel repeated, looking at Frank.

"Oh, you needn't worry; she said nothing uncomplimentary about you. She said nothing uncomplimentary about anyone, in fact." His friend sounded a little disappointed.

"Really, Frank." Nathaniel shook his head. "These people are not your playthings, you know."

"Am I to have two lectures in one evening?" Frank exclaimed. Then, as Mrs Seymour and Letty emerged from the door with a sullen manservant holding an umbrella above their heads, Frank added, with a sigh, "Nate, I know they're not. Besides, if I were searching for a plaything, I don't think I should choose Demelza Abbott. She is far too forbidding."

"Be careful," said Nathaniel, and leaned back with a start as Frank reached out to ruffle his wet hair. "What—what are you..."

"Why should I be careful?" Frank was laughing.

"Boys, boys," said Mrs Seymour good-humouredly, as she and Letty came up. "Do try to behave like gentlemen."

Later on, as they were going to their rooms in the Grange, Frank said thoughtfully, "She's not exactly pretty, is she? Demelza Abbott."

Nathaniel just shrugged. Not seeming to need any more confirmation, Frank went on, eagerly keeping pace with him, "Gertrude White, now, she's pretty. Dark hair, roses in her cheeks—she's much more my idea of a woman."

"I quite agree," said Nathaniel. But his friend was not finished.

"All the same, there is something about Miss Abbott: something that's not quite prettiness, or beauty, but a kind of a—a light. In the way she speaks and looks. Am I making any sense?"

"No." Nathaniel sighed, and turned toward his room, where the light burning under his door showed that his valet was waiting. "Goodnight, Frank."

∽

The dinner party was hailed as a success by all, but before Demelza could drag her weary feet to her room, Mrs White took her aside, her flowery perfume wafting in her nostrils.

"I know you must be exhausted, my dear, but I just thought I might give you a little hint, not to put yourself forward too much on these occasions."

"Aunt Josephine," Demelza said, in some confusion. "I don't..."

"It is very tempting, I am sure," Mrs White went on, "when a handsome young man such as Mr Honeychurch shows you some attention. And I'm sure it must be difficult not to lose your head. But you must not dominate him as you did tonight, Demelza. You see, Miss Seymour and Gertrude were neglected as a result."

"I didn't—that is, I don't think..."

"I'm sure you understand just what I mean, my dear. And I don't need to explain to you the difference in your positions." As Demelza looked down, Mrs White patted her shoulder. "Go along to bed now, my dear. I thought it would be good for you to have that hint; that is all."

On her way upstairs, Demelza glanced at the baize door that led to the servants' quarters and paused. She thought again of Cecil's dark, watchful eyes at dinner, of his pale face in the darkness when she had surprised him and the girl.

"Demi? What are you doing?" Gertrude came up beside her and glanced at the door. "Are you looking for someone?"

"Just—Cecil," said Demelza, with a shake of her head.

"Cecil? At this hour?"

"Well, I just wanted to ask him something. But it can wait till morning." And with a gentle goodnight, Demelza ascended the stairs to her gable room, and did not notice the smile that crossed the other young lady's face.

The world was white and dreadful when Ivy Kent walked to work early the next morning. The packet Cecil had given her was burning a hole in her pocket. She thought, at every corner she turned, that a police constable would jump out and point his finger at her. But none did. She did see a minister crossing Main Street, and it nearly made her turn back home.

But Ivy went on. She opened the shop door of the haberdasher's with her key, climbed the stairs, and built a fire in the sitting room. At half-past seven, she brought Mr Jorkins—who was already up and working—his tea and was proud of the fact that her hands did not tremble as she handed him the cup.

Later, she retched in the back yard of the haberdasher's and wiped her streaming eyes with her apron before going back inside.

5

A MEDICAL MAN

On the morning after their visit to Highfield House, a meeting had been scheduled with the land manager and agent, and just as she had done so successfully last time, Mrs Seymour gently advised her son to go and entertain his guest while she went to the meeting. Or perhaps her gentle advice might have been better termed as an outright order.

She ought to have felt guilty for domineering her son in this way, Clara knew. He had always been gentle, unlike his father, and that made it easier to direct him. But could she really be blamed for wanting to be at the centre of things? Her daughter's coming-out was in just a few days, and the best way to ensure that the ship sailed smoothly was to commandeer the wheel herself. Clara had never been to sea, of course, but she felt sure that a naval captain would have sympathised with her position.

The meeting was in the library, a room that was seldom used these days now that John was gone. They sat for a few minutes waiting for Jorkins, who was late, and Clara could feel herself growing more anxious. She could not help recalling her rudeness yesterday. He had spoken to her almost as a friend, and she had responded by putting distance between them. Suppose he did not come today? Suppose whatever tentative thing had been growing between them had been nipped in the bud by her own actions?

"Mrs Seymour," said Parsons, shifting in his seat. "I think we had better begin without Mr Jorkins. It is just the new cottages I wanted to discuss, in any case: we still plan to have three built at the end of the year..."

"Ah, Mrs Simms!" Mrs Seymour cried as her housekeeper appeared at the door, grateful for the interruption. "Come in."

"I wished to go over the menu for the ball with you, ma'am, but it can wait until after the meeting..."

"No, no, we may as well discuss it now as we are waiting for Jorkins." Clara heard Parsons sigh, almost inaudibly, and turned to address him. "I'm sorry, Parsons, this is his project too, is it not? I'm sure he has just been delayed: we ought to give him a chance to arrive."

"Yes, ma'am," he said, frowning down at his papers with an air of resignation. Mrs Simms came up to her mistress's elbow, and they had just started discussing appetisers when the footman stepped in to announce Mr Jorkins.

They all stared at the land agent as he came in. He looked as though he had been up all night. His eyes were bloodshot, the skin under them pouchy, and his skin was pale and waxy. When he spoke, his voice was unmeasurably weary. "Apologies for the delay, Mrs Seymour. I hope I have not kept you waiting for too long."

"Jorkins..." Clara said, and did not feel capable of saying anything else for the moment. She had risen automatically, forcing Parsons to do the same. Mrs Simms was rooted to the spot, staring at Mr Jorkins. "Are you..."

"I have been working on the plans for the cottages, ma'am," Mr Jorkins continued, as though unaware that they were all staring at him. He rooted in the bag he had brought with him and set the plans down on the table. "If you wish, I can detail the various changes I have made, to contribute to a more efficient—structure..." He stopped, and his body began to shake, as though some silent convulsion had seized him. Taking one step back and then another, he reached into his pocket for a handkerchief and began to cough.

"Mr Jorkins," said Clara, coming to his side and trying to speak as sternly as possible, which was difficult as she could feel her heart give a curious twist inside her chest. "You are very ill. You ought not to have come to work today."

"I am—sorry—ma'am..." He spoke between coughs, and turned away from her, but not before she saw the blood spotting his handkerchief. Clara drew in a deep breath and told herself to stay calm. She put a hand to Mr Jorkins's shoulder and turned back to Mrs Simms and Mr Parsons.

"Parsons, we'd better have this meeting at another time, when Mr Jorkins is feeling better. Mrs Simms, would you send a message to our doctor to come attend Mr Jorkins?"

"No—no," Mr Jorkins said. He had stopped coughing now, and his voice was firm. "No, ma'am, you are very kind, but I shall go home and rest. If my condition gets any worse, I can send my maid to summon a surgeon."

"It is no trouble, Jorkins," said Clara, but a little weakly: she could feel the curious stares of the others in the room and knew that she ought to be masking her emotions a little better.

"Thank you, Mrs Seymour. I am sure I will be better soon. I am sorry..." Mr Jorkins looked around for the first time, and some colour returned to his cheeks, as though he were willing himself to feel better, "I am sorry to have alarmed you all."

"Very well, but you must take our carriage. Parsons, can you see that he gets there safely?" Clara watched, wringing her hands, as they left the library, and stood staring at the door until she had heard their voices fade away down the corridor. Then, at the sound of a clearing of a throat, she realised that her housekeeper was still in the room. "Oh—sorry, Mrs Simms. Let us look at the menu now."

Mr Quigley spent the day visiting clients, and when he came back an hour before dinner, he marched straight downstairs. He passed through the kitchen, ignored the bemused bows of the maid and cook, and found Cecil in the pantry organising the shelves.

"Leave that," he told his valet, shutting the door of the cellar behind them. "She didn't give him enough."

"What do you mean, sir?"

"Your little friend, whom you told me you could rely on. She evidently did not give Mr Quigley a high enough dosage, for he was still walking around town when I saw him this morning."

"Oh, yes, that." Cecil's head dipped. He rose to his feet, drawing in a deep breath. "I was going to tell you, sir—"

"Going to tell me what? That she would let us down? That she was not capable of doing the job? Well, evidently it is too late for that now." Mr Quigley ran a hand through his hair. He was really agitated; he did not like for his servants to see him like this, least of all Cecil, with his sly eyes. "You had better tread carefully, Simms, or you'll receive nothing of what I promised you."

"Sir," began Cecil, matching his master's low volume, "You did say so yourself, that the type of poison we used—might take longer depending on the person. Mr Jorkins is a strong man, stronger, perhaps, than we might have realised..."

"And the longer he is ill, the more time he has to suspect us of foul play; the more time he has to dig into our affairs! I thought I had made myself very clear, Simms. I told you that I wanted him dead." Mr Quigley wound down, staring at the valet. "Why are you so calm?"

"Because, sir," said Cecil, taking a cautious step forward, "I think I know how we can make this better."

"I am all ears."

"My mother visits me here every Wednesday, you know, sir. Well, today, she had something rather interesting to tell me." Cecil paused. His master watched him in cold silence. "She told me that Mr Jorkins came to a meeting at the Grange this morning, and Mrs Seymour was very anxious when she saw his evident ill health."

"I fail to see how this improves matters, Cecil, since the more people who know about Mr Jorkins's condition, the worse it will be for us. Now, I cannot waste my time here any longer..."

"But my mother, sir, thinks there might be something between them."

Mr Quigley paused with his back to Cecil, his hand on the door. Slowly he turned. "Between Mrs Seymour and Mr Jorkins?"

"Mrs Seymour wanted to summon her family doctor to attend to him, sir," said Cecil, each word laden with extra significance as his dark eyes gleamed. "Mr Jorkins refused, said he would send for one instead if he got any worse."

"Hmph." Mr Quigley was silent for a minute or two. At last he looked up at Cecil, considering. "Then perhaps all is not lost after all."

～

Demelza had spent all day after the Seymours' visit searching for Cecil, to no avail. Every time she ventured downstairs, it was always to find that he had just stepped out, and since she had a dread of going near her stepfather's room, she was not likely to seek out his valet there. Accordingly, on Thursday morning, she went into Hartleton at an early hour to post some more letters, and stopped at Johnson's, as she had heard from one of the townspeople that her uncle was staying there.

The shop door of the haberdasher's was locked, and she knocked on it tentatively. The upstairs window, when she glanced up, had its curtains closed firmly within it. Feeling the beginnings of alarm, Demelza knocked harder, and called out, "Mr Jorkins? Mr Jorkins!"

She was beginning to attract stares from a few passersby when at last the door was wrenched open. A maidservant was standing there, the same girl whom Demelza had seen talking to Cecil the other day. She raised her eyebrows and looked Demelza up and down, from her black bonnet to her scuffed boots. "Yes?"

"I was hoping to call on my uncle," Demelza said, a little thrown off by the girl's clear lack of embarrassment. She went on, half-bluffing, "I wanted to... invite him to dinner at my stepfather's house..."

"Mr Jorkins is sleeping," said the maid. "He's a little under the weather."

"Under the weather? Why—what's the matter with him?"

"I'm sure I don't know, miss. But I'll tell him you called. Good day." And just like that, the maid shut the door in Demelza's face. A moment later, she heard the key turning in the lock.

Inside the stairwell, Ivy Kent leaned her back against the door, and caught her breath. She did not feel that she could move again until she heard Demelza's footsteps receding from the door. Then, finally, she climbed the stairs and resumed sweeping the landing, with eyes that were beginning to blur with tears.

"Ivy? Ivy?" A voice, thin and reedy, issued from the closed door to Mr Jorkins's bedroom. Ivy went in reluctantly, blinking away her tears.

"What is it, sir?"

Hugh Jorkins lay in bed. The curtains to his window were closed, but through the dim light that issued through a gap in between them, she could see that his forehead was covered in sweat. He was breathing heavily. "Was there someone... at the door? Ivy? I thought I heard knocking."

"No, sir, that was next door. Will I get you some more water?"

"No... thank you." Mr Jorkins settled back on his pillows and closed his eyes. Ivy went to the window, and looked down through the gap, flinching back when she saw that Demelza was still standing in the street. She tugged the curtains closed and fastened them.

~

It was a sunny June day, which had brought many people from all over the valley to Hartleton. Gertrude and Demelza joined these crowds, to make some purchases for the ball on Saturday. Gertrude's dress, of course, had already been bought and made, and Demelza had decided that she would wear her grey silk, but there were still sashes and ribbons to be bought, and many other things that Demelza had not even considered, but that her companion certainly had.

Small boxes began to pile up in Demelza's arms as they moved from shop to shop. Gertrude thanked her every now and then, of course, and reminded Cecil, whom Mrs White had assigned to help them, to carry his share. But he seemed to have a very deft way of getting out of things, and often he would disappear for up to half an hour, only to reappear when they were straggling up the street with one of the shop assistants trailing behind them.

The second time this happened, Demelza passed a particularly heavy bandbox into Cecil's hands and thanked him as she adjusted her grip on her own load. When Gertrude disappeared into the milliner's, Demelza took the opportunity of addressing Cecil. He was scanning the passersby with a bored expression.

"I went to see Mr Jorkins this morning."

"Oh?" He raised his dark eyebrows and looked at her in mild surprise. "And how did you manage that? I'm sure I didn't see you go."

"I left very early. I walked in and out."

"Well. Aren't you wonderful." Cecil's voice was laden with sarcasm, and he was looking off to the side once more. Demelza took a step closer, her gaze fixed on his face.

"He's ill. And I think you've got something to do with it. I heard what you said the other day—I saw you with that girl, his maid..."

"Ivy," said Cecil, who had not so much as flinched. "She happens to be a very good friend of mine. More than a friend, actually—oh, you're not jealous, Demi, are you?"

"Stop talking nonsense." Demelza's voice was low and fervent. "Tell me what's going on. Tell me what you've got yourself mixed up in, Cecil, or I will make sure everyone at home knows about this—the Whites and—and my stepfather, too..."

The flash of mirth in Cecil's eyes came and went quickly, but Demelza ground to a halt, staring at him. "What? What's so funny about what I just said?"

"Nothing," he said, quickly.

"Mr Quigley knows about this, doesn't he?" Demelza said slowly. "And the Whites, too?" She reached for his arm. "Cecil..."

"Listen to me." The valet stepped right into her space, closing his hand over hers and pressing down so hard that Demelza winced. "Whatever you think you know, it doesn't matter. Because no one listens to you, anyway, do they?" He smiled, right up close. "So you can go running around asking people about your uncle, saying that Mr Quigley has done something, and no one will even bat an eyelid. Your mother was nothing and you are nothing—"

The sound of the shop door swinging open startled them, and Cecil dropped Demelza's arm so fast that a couple of the boxes tumbled from her arms to the pavement. "Oh, I'm sorry!" said Gertrude. She had a rather strange smile on her face and spoke very pointedly as she looked from one of them to the other. "Did I interrupt something?"

"Nothing, Miss White," said Cecil quickly, and he bent down to help Demelza pick up the things. She avoided his gaze, and was reaching for the box of ribbons when a gloved hand closed over it, and a familiar voice said,

"Allow me."

Demelza was helped to her feet and looked up into the pale blue eyes of Nathaniel Seymour.

Frank Honeychurch was evidently not as charmed by provincial life as he kept proclaiming to be, since for the last two days now he had had supplies from town delivered to Hartleton's post office. On both occasions, he had dragged Nathaniel with him to pick up these all-important deliveries, which seemed to consist of things like cravats and creams and hair powder (Nathaniel had opened one of the boxes yesterday, earning him a scolding from his friend).

"I just don't understand why you have to send to Bond Street for a hat, or a neckcloth, or a collar," said Nathaniel now, gesturing to the shop windows they were passing. "Things you can just as easily get here."

Frank gave him a withering look, tucking the packages under one arm. "If you really see no difference, Nate, between this..." He gestured down at his blue frock coat and tanned trousers, then to his friend's dark, heavy coat and white neckcloth, "Then there is no hope for you. Goodness, I must take you to town."

"I don't like town," Nathaniel muttered.

"You're lucky you have a pretty face, then." Frank clapped him on the shoulder, laughing, and then stopped short. "Oh, look, your friends." He pointed across the street, to where Miss White, Miss Abbott and a servant were outside the milliner's. Miss Abbott had just dropped some boxes on the pavement, and the servant was helping her. Nathaniel had crossed the street before Frank even said another word.

"Allow me," he said, and helped Demelza to her feet. She looked up at him, and there was a fierceness in her eyes which took him aback. But it softened and faded after a moment as she continued to look at him, and Nathaniel felt oddly relieved to find that he was not its object—whatever it was.

Gertrude White, anxious to explain, came to hover at his elbow as he began to gather up the boxes that had fallen. "We've been shopping all morning and we've bought ever so many things for your sister's ball. I think we might have gotten a little carried away, though—you see, we walked here, and I don't see how we're going to walk back now with all of these things."

"Didn't I see you here earlier this morning?" said Frank to Demelza as he came up to them. "Sorry, I would help with those boxes, but as you can see my hands are full."

Nathaniel gathered up the last box and turned to raise his eyebrows at his friend. "You mean to tell me you've been to the post office already today?"

"Of course! I had to check if my things had arrived," said Frank, with a shrug.

"I'm afraid that my friend," said Nathaniel to the ladies, as he straightened, "is incurably vain." They heard a snort and saw that it had come from the manservant behind Demelza, who quickly took on a blank expression under their gazes.

"But if I am to understand Frank and Miss White," Nathaniel went on, turning to Demelza, "then you have already had a lot of walking today, Miss Abbott. May I offer you our carriage?"

She began to protest; Miss White, however, got there first, declaring that they couldn't possibly accept as there was not enough room.

"That is easily remedied," Nathaniel said, calmly, with a glance at his friend. "We can walk back to the Grange."

"Walk?" Frank repeated in his friend's ear, and then, addressing the ladies with a smile, "Yes, of course we can walk. One of the great advantages of country living, after all, are its great walks, or so I hear."

"You shall learn the truth of that soon enough," said Nathaniel, and the party started along the pavement, toward the church where the carriage was waiting.

It was soon necessary for them to split into pairs. The manservant dropped a good distance behind, and Gertrude seemed to be about to speak to Nathaniel when Frank came up to offer her his arm. With a glance backward, she had no choice but to go, and Nathaniel and Demelza fell into step together.

To his surprise, she spoke first. "I must thank you, Mr Seymour, for your kindness, though I'm sure it is not necessary."

"I'm sure that it is," he countered, with a sidelong glance at her. She was walking heavily, and there were shadows under her eyes as though she had not slept. "You ought not to exert yourself so much."

"My aunt always has errands for me."

"Well, can't she send a servant?" Demelza gave a half-smile at this, and Nathaniel looked back over his shoulder to the sullen manservant, who was glaring at their backs. "On second thought, perhaps not."

She glanced back, too, and then seemed to come to a decision. "There is something I must tell you, Mr Seymour." By the urgency in her tone, Nathaniel thought he could guess what she was going to say.

"Please, Miss Abbott, you must allow me to speak first." He stared up at the sky for a moment, though no divine inspiration came, and he was forced to go along with his own plodding apology. "I have been... unforgivably rude, since you arrived back in Hartleton. I cannot explain why, but you must understand that it had nothing to do with you." He glanced toward her. She was looking down at the pavement, and a strand of blonde hair had fallen over her eyes so that he could not see their expression. "And that our friendship is something that I have missed."

"Were we friends?" she said, and though others might have asked such a question in a different way, there was no taint of bitterness to her tone: only delighted surprise, which touched Nathaniel right to the heart. He could not help smiling.

"Yes, Miss Abbott. And I should like to be again."

"Then you mustn't call me Miss Abbott anymore, but Demelza."

"Only if you will call me Nathaniel." He glanced ahead, toward where Frank and Miss White were walking. "Or Nate. Though I think Frank is the only one who calls me Nate."

"Then I wouldn't like to deny him the privilege," Demelza said, a smile in her voice. But he could feel her anxious glance, and she seemed to want to say something else. At that moment, however, Gertrude dropped Frank's arm and turned back in some exasperation, joining them so that they could not continue their conversation. Frank raised his eyebrows at Nathaniel and shrugged his shoulders as though to say, I don't know what I did.

They handed the young ladies into the carriage, followed by their array of purchases. The manservant knocked Nathaniel's shoulders as he brushed past him and hopped up on the seat with the driver.

"Well," said Frank, watching the carriage wistfully. "You seem unaccountably cheerful. Do you really love country walks so much? Or is it simply that you take pleasure in my suffering?"

"Both," said Nathaniel, after pretending to consider for a moment. Grinning, he pushed his friend on. "Come on, we'd better start now if we want to be back by nightfall."

Mrs White's surprise on seeing the Seymours' carriage pull up outside Highfield House was so great that she had to rush out to greet the young ladies. Cecil jumped down from the carriage and slunk away, looking up once to nod to his master, who was watching from the window of the library.

Mr Quigley turned back into the room. "It is all settled, I think."

"All settled? Good, good," said Mr White, with a nervous laugh; seeing the look on his brother-in-law's face, however, he quickly turned it into a cough, and stuffed his hands in the pockets of his waistcoat. "So, James, you trust this man, then?"

"Mr Thomas is a good and loyal friend. He will do whatever I ask of him."

"Good, good," said Mr White again, and then a moment later, "But you must admit, James, that it is a little risky."

"Business is risk, Geoffrey."

"Yes, I do follow you—but this isn't exactly business, is it? It's more of a family affair, considering that Mr Jorkins is Esther's—"

"Don't," said Mr Quigley, in a voice that cut like glass, "mention her name. I have told you before, Geoffrey."

"Yes, of course, I am sorry, James..."

Mr Quigley ignored his blustering, passing out of the library to find Cecil climbing the stairs. He gestured to his valet, who followed him into his bedroom.

"So Mr Thomas is to be summoned to attend Mr Jorkins, then, as we planned?"

"Yes, sir." Cecil removed his master's day coat and went to get his tails. "I managed to get away to meet Ivy while I was in town with Miss White and Miss Abbott, and she agreed to do it. It might look strange to some, hiring a strange surgeon, but then Mr Jorkins has no close relatives apart from Miss Abbott and—" He stopped, as though he had just realised something. Mr Quigley, following his own train of thought, went on,

"What about Mrs Seymour? If your mother is to be believed, then Mrs Seymour seems to take a great interest in Mr Jorkins's welfare." He couldn't help smiling a little at that fact; it had been such a surprising and useful bit of intelligence. He was sure it would pay dividends too, in due time.

"I thought of that, too, sir, and I've spoken to my mother. She will make sure to put in a good word for Mr Thomas, so that Mrs Seymour doesn't take anything amiss." As Mr Quigley looked around, sharply, Cecil helped him on with his dinner coat and added, "She doesn't know anything either, sir. My mother, that is. She does what I tell her."

"I should hope so," said Mr Quigley, adjusting his lapels and brushing off an imaginary speck of dust. "And I should hope that is the case with Ivy, too. Or is that what is troubling you, Cecil?"

He turned around to face his valet, who visibly swallowed. "No, sir. It's not Ivy I'm worried about. It's Miss Abbott."

"Demelza?" Mr Quigley repeated. He shook his head, and removed his glasses, passing them to Cecil. "That child is no cause for worry. She hasn't even met her uncle since he got back—I made sure of that."

"She has met him, sir," Cecil said, uncomfortably, as he rubbed the lenses with a cloth. Under his master's stare, "And she has tried to visit him at least once, since he has been ill. Mrs White sends her into town on errands early every morning."

"Does she?" With a dry laugh, "Well, that ends now. Pass me my glasses, Cecil. I'm not about to let that child poke her nose into my affairs."

∽

Demelza gazed out of her gable window. A golden haze lay over the valley, which would soon morph into grey and then deepen into dark blue. She had become familiar with the beauty of Hartleton sunsets. But she watched the valley this evening with a quivering sort of attention, aware that Nathaniel was somewhere down in it, and no matter how many times she told herself not to get carried away, no matter how the worries about her uncle and stepfather and Cecil had wound themselves into her mind, she could not help smiling every time she thought of their meeting.

He had said that he wanted to be friends again. She knew that she must not take her own interpretation of that, and run on ahead in her mind, thinking of their future together, but all the same, it was difficult to curb the instinct.

When the door to her gable room crashed open on its hinges, Demelza was roused from her pleasant trance, and turned to see her stepfather standing on the threshold. He was dressed for dinner. For a moment, the light of the setting sun gleamed in his glasses and made them into two whorls of gold. "Mr—Mr Quigley?" The gold faded: his dark gaze cut her down where she stood, and she looked around wildly for the source of his anger; she closed the window and reached for her shawl. "Am I needed downstairs? Has something happened?"

"Be quiet," said her stepfather. "You know what this is, I imagine?" He reached into the pocket of his waistcoat and drew out a key. "I am going to lock this door. And you are going to stay here and be quiet, until you have learned not to interfere in matters that do not concern you."

Demelza stared; she flung herself forward a moment too late and found herself beating her fists against a closed door. The handle only gave a half-turn; the hinges groaned but did not give. She leaned her forehead against the cool wood and listened to her stepfather's footsteps fade away down the stairs.

6

IN WRITING

W hen Mrs Seymour went into town the next morning, it was to find, with a sinking dismay, that Mr Hugh Jorkins was no better: that, in fact, he was a good deal worse now than he had been two days ago. He was not conscious, but his shallow breathing and fluttering eyelids made it clear that he was not enjoying a peaceful sleep, either. Her only comfort was in the maid's assertion that the doctor had been summoned and would arrive soon.

"It seems, Mrs Seymour, that there is nothing more you can do for the moment," said Frank Honeychurch from the doorway. He had paled at the sight of the sick man, and lingered on the threshold, as though to take one step into the room would be to expose himself to contagion. Clara Seymour had no such qualms; she had taken a seat by Mr Jorkins's bedside, and was gazing at the tough, callused hand that lay on top of his bedspread. The fingers twitched every now and then, as though he were about to wake up, but his eyes would not focus on any object for long and soon drifted back into unconsciousness.

"I am not leaving until I have seen the doctor," said Clara, firmly. With a glance at the young man, "Though that is no reason to keep you here, Frank." In fact, she did not know why he insisted on accompanying her in the first place. Was it simply because Nathaniel had been intent on going to call on the Whites by himself?

Seeming to guess what was going through her head, Frank shifted from one foot to the other. His gaze flickered to Mr Jorkins, and he grimaced. "The man is Miss Abbott's uncle, is he not?"

"Yes," said Clara, warily.

"Then I shall wait, too."

They watched one another for a moment, and Clara was the first to break the silence. "Frank, I know it is not my place, but I think perhaps I ought to warn you."

"Warn me, madam?"

"Miss Abbott is a deserving girl, I am sure." Clara looked around the room, but her mind was suddenly far away. "As was her mother, Esther. She was Nathaniel and Letty's governess when they were younger, you know." She glanced back at Frank, who looked unsurprised. "And Demelza will likely follow in her mother's footsteps. She has no fortune, Frank."

"But her father was a businessman, wasn't he?" At Mrs Seymour's raised eyebrows, "Miss Abbott told me."

"Mr Abbott was in trade," Clara conceded, "but he ran into financial trouble not long before his death. His warehouse was on the point of closing down—were it not for my husband and Mr Quigley's investments after Mr Abbott died, it would have been run into the ground. Now Mr White runs it."

"So mightn't they do something for her? For Miss Abbott?" There was an eagerness in Frank's eyes which disgusted Clara a little. She was not really surprised; London was full of fortune-hunters, after all. It was just a pity that her son had to befriend one and bring him into their lives.

"No," she said coolly, turning back to Mr Jorkins. "I am sure Mr White will not. Mr Quigley, I imagine, would not want to leave his stepdaughter destitute after his death, but he will probably live for a great many years yet, so in the meantime she must work. You had better look elsewhere, Mr Honeychurch."

Not long after that, the maid came to the door to announce the arrival of the surgeon. They heard a heavy tread come up the corridor, and then Mr Thomas barrelled in. He was well-built, looked to be in his fifties, and had a greying moustache which quivered expressively as he looked first at Frank, then at Mrs Seymour, and finally at the patient.

"Well, well! Mrs Seymour and her son, I suppose. I see that Mr Jorkins has plenty of friends who are anxious about his welfare. That is a comfort to a man, I am sure. But I must respectfully request that you allow me space to work. Miracles, you know, require a little time."

"Mr Thomas," said Clara, who had risen to her feet. She did not bother correcting him about Frank. "What do you think is the matter with him?"

"Well, it is difficult to say, you know. I saw him first yesterday evening upon my arrival here. A most charming town, Hartleton," Mr Thomas added, with a glance back at Frank, who nodded in agreement. "In any case, it is difficult to make any pronouncements until I have observed him for a little longer."

"Observed him?" Clara repeated, and the urgency in her tone drew curious glances from both of her companions, and even from the maid hovering behind Frank. She hastily regulated her tones. "I beg your pardon, Mr Thomas, but surely something must be done beyond that?"

"Well, yes, yes, of course, ma'am," said the surgeon, with the same indulgent air by which one might address an over-excited child. He set down his bag by Mr Jorkins's bedside and began to rummage inside. "The first thing, of course, that must be done is to break his fever. And now, begging your pardon, I must be allowed a little time to work alone."

"I would be grateful," said Clara, when she and Frank were outside, "if you would not mention to anyone my... excessive alarm. Mr Jorkins is a good worker, and I should be sorry to lose him, you see, but I know that my fear might be misinterpreted..."

"Your secret is safe with me, madam," said Frank, solemnly, and she glanced at him in annoyance.

"It is not a secret. A secret implies—something sordid. I am just asking for a little discretion: that is all."

"In return, Mrs Seymour," said Frank, after a short pause, "would you not mention to anyone my interest in Miss Abbott's welfare? I fear that might be misinterpreted, too."

"I am not bargaining with you," said Mrs Clara Seymour, crossly, and she picked up her stride on the way to the carriage until Frank had to run to keep up with her.

Nathaniel had insisted on visiting Highfield House by himself because it was Demelza whom he wished to see, and though he had meant it when he told her the day before that he wanted to be friends, he was not quite ready to introduce the subject to his mother yet. As for Frank, Nathaniel's reservations tended in quite another direction.

But he might as well have brought them along, as it turned out, for when Mr Quigley's valet showed him into the drawing room, he was greeted with the delighted faces of Mrs White and Gertrude.

"Where is Miss Abbott?" he asked, as soon as civility allowed him. The mother and daughter exchanged a quick glance before the latter answered,

"Poor Demi has a headache this morning. But you are very kind to worry about her, Mr Seymour."

"It is nothing serious, I hope?"

"Oh! No. That child is always coming down with something or another." With another significant glance at her daughter, Mrs White rose to her feet. "Well! I'd better see what is delaying the tea."

When she was out of the room, Gertrude leaned forward confidentially. "I am so excited for your sister's ball, Mr Seymour. I haven't been able to think of anything else."

"Yes," he said, his mind still distracted. "I mean—thank you. I hope it is a good occasion."

"Do you know that Mr Honeychurch tried to get me to save him the first dance? I told him that I had already promised another gentleman. That is, unless I am mistaken in thinking..."

At the first note of anxiety in her tone, Nathaniel snapped back to attention. "Yes, yes of course," he said. "I should still like to dance with you first, if I may."

Gertrude dimpled: her whole face seemed to clear, like a sun coming out from behind the clouds. She was very pretty, Nathaniel reflected, not for the first time, with her full lips and her neat black curls and her long dark eyelashes. He recalled his mother saying that she might have had her pick of any young bachelor in the neighbourhood. Why was it that he suddenly wished he were not one of the few young bachelors in the neighbourhood?

"I hope Demi will be able to go, too," Gertrude went on, with a sigh. "I am so fond of her, you know. I don't know how I managed before she came here."

"Your mother said that she is often ill?"

A faint wrinkle marred the perfect smoothness of Gertrude's brow. She considered for a moment, and then said, "Yes, poor Demi. But between you and me, Mr Seymour, I'm not sure I believe she has a headache. I think she might be suffering from some other ailment. An ailment of the heart. I think you understand my meaning."

She could not have made herself plainer if she had tried. Nathaniel cleared his throat, sitting forward in his chair. "Then—you think there is someone whom Miss Abbott prefers?"

"Oh, I couldn't possibly say for sure," said Gertrude, looking away with a bashful air. "Every young lady has her secrets, you know."

"But do you think..." Nathaniel was trying to make his voice as casual as possible, as he could feel her curious gaze. But there was no stopping now; his mind had leapt forward and was considering all the awful possibilities. "If there were such a young man, that is—do you think he would be worthy of her?"

Gertrude was silent for a moment or two, her hands curved on the arms of her chair. "If it is who I am thinking of," she said at last, "then I am sure Demelza could not have chosen anyone better."

Nathaniel swallowed. There was another anxious question on his lips when Mrs White returned from an errand, and thus followed a painful half-hour of unrelated conversation before he could extricate himself. As he returned to the Grange on horseback, his mind kept replaying every moment that he had witnessed between Frank and Demelza, as though it were intent on torturing him.

It was good to be reunited with friends, and it was even better when those friends had returned to one's life in some useful capacity. Accordingly, Mr Quigley felt very cheerful when he met Percival Thomas outside his house. His mood darkened again, however, when he saw a pale face looking down at him from the gable window.

"Who's that little creature?" said Mr Thomas, following Mr Quigley's gaze.

"I shall tell you later. I shall tell you all about her." But the first thing Mr Quigley did when they got into the house was to tell Cecil to go up and check on Demelza. Once he was satisfied that she was still in her room and hadn't been seen by anyone (it seemed Mr Seymour had called upon the house only an hour or so before), he led his old friend to the library.

"So, how is our patient?"

"Not very well, unfortunately," replied Mr Thomas, putting on a grave countenance. "As a medical man, you know, James..."

"A medical man, yes, quite—"

"I should not give him more than a day to live."

"That is sorry news indeed." Mr Quigley paused, and glanced at the curtains, which had been partly closed over the window. In a sudden flash of movement, he darted forward and yanked the curtains back. They drifted and settled, and Mr Quigley blinked.

His friend was laughing. "What on earth was that, James? Did you think someone was hiding there?"

"No," Mr Quigley said, quickly and resentfully. He folded his arms and fixed his friend with a hard stare, until he had settled down. "But you're sure you have given him enough?"

"Enough to put him under. It is slow-acting stuff, though, James, as you know. But this way it will arouse less suspicion —it will look like he passed in his sleep, and the coroner's report..."

"Never mind the coroner's report," snapped Mr Quigley. "I have managed such things before. I can do it again."

Mr Thomas blew out his cheeks. "Very well, then. I shall make sure to give him a higher dosage tomorrow. I should get myself far away though, until it has all blown over."

"Yes, that would probably be wise." Mr Quigley paused, surveying his friend for a moment, and then, "About that, Percy."

"Yes?"

"Well, I have my own family troubles, you know, and I have been thinking of a way that we might—pardon the expression—kill two birds with one stone."

❧

Gertrude was vaguely aware that Demelza was in some disgrace, and this had necessitated a half-lie to Nathaniel Seymour when he had come calling earlier that day. But in her own mind, there was no falsehood in what she had told him relating to Demelza's heart; she really, sincerely believed that it belonged to a certain young man, and this belief had come about through careful observation over the past week.

She had caught Demelza and Cecil more than once, after all, in what looked like an intimate moment. Demelza seemed to know Cecil better than she knew anyone else. A particular incident that stood out in Gertrude's memory was when she had come out of the milliner's yesterday to find them holding hands. The touch had been so brief, of course, that the gentlemen who soon joined them afterward did not seem to have noticed anything. Indeed, if Nathaniel's reaction today was anything to go by, he hadn't had any idea that Demelza's heart was engaged—which gave Gertrude a little concern, but she thought perhaps he was offended at the notion of a young lady falling in love with a servant. Gertrude, for her part, found it rather romantic.

It was for this reason that when Mrs White, arranging her daughter's hair for dinner, dropped some hint about Mr Quigley's plans for Demelza, Gertrude turned to look at her in horror.

"Mr Thomas?" she repeated.

"I thought you'd be pleased, my dear," said her mother, very mildly. "And Demelza ought to be, as well. This means that she won't have to hire herself out."

"He must be fifty, at least—Mummy, you cannot be serious."

"I am always serious, my dear." Mrs White bristled at the implication that her words could ever be taken lightly. "Mr Thomas is James's old friend, and he is looking for a wife.

She may not be as pretty as you, Gertrude, but she is capable of holding her tongue and doing her duty, I suppose, and that is important to a man of Mr Thomas's—where are you going, my dear?"

"To speak to Uncle James," said Gertrude, hurrying for the door with her hair half-down, half-up. Ignoring her mother's protesting voice, she crossed the corridor, ran down to the first-floor landing, and knocked frantically on her uncle's door.

Cecil was tying his master's cravat when Gertrude came in. She stared at him for a moment, and then said, "Uncle, I must speak to you alone."

"Certainly, Gertrude," said Mr Quigley, and he regarded her curiously as Cecil left the room. "Why, whatever is the matter?"

"Mummy just told me what you're planning." Her uncle's eyes narrowed, which made Gertrude all the more defiant. "You can't just marry Demelza off to your friend like that, uncle, you just can't."

"Ah, so this is about Demelza and Mr Thomas."

"What else would it be about?" Gertrude exclaimed. "You can't make her do it, uncle."

"Of course, I cannot make her do anything. But what other prospects does she have? I think she would prefer to live a comfortable life than to be shafted from household to household, teaching ungrateful children." Mr Quigley paused, and then added, almost as an afterthought, "And to tell the truth, I am much more easy knowing that Demelza is in good hands. One hears such stories about the way governesses are treated..."

"You don't understand!" cried Gertrude, taking a step forward. Her uncle looked her up and down, evidently alarmed by her sudden burst of emotion. "She is in love with someone else, uncle."

Mr Quigley's lips twitched, as though he were trying not to smile. "I think, Gertrude, that this is a conversation we can have at another time."

"Don't you care who she's in love with?" Gertrude reached for him, and he moved quickly, taking hold of her arm and marching her to the door. "Don't you care if she's unhappy?"

"I think, Gertrude dear," said Mr Quigley, "that you have been reading too many books. Whatever romantic notions you might have about that child, I would advise you to cast them away now. Her fate is mine to decide."

When Nathaniel got back to the Grange, it took him some time to locate Frank. His mother had gone out again, and Letty was no help. Apparently, choosing which necklace she ought to wear for the ball was more pressing business than helping her brother find his friend and prevent him from breaking a good girl's heart.

At length, one of the servants told him that he had seen Mr Honeychurch walking in the grounds, and so Nathaniel burst out of the house with his riding clothes still on. Afternoon was stretching into evening, and the wood was alive and breathing, reaching its green arms down to Nathaniel. He met his friend coming up the main path.

"Nate, you're back! Yes, it's true: I've been so bored in your absence that I've actually started walking. Walking! As though our forced march yesterday weren't enough to turn me off it forever. But I saw the most enchanting little cabin back there, Nate..." Frank turned, pointing through the trees. "It seems to have been abandoned for a few years, but you could renovate it as a rustic cottage—you know that's quite in style at the moment. I know a few fellows who have undertaken similar projects..."

"Frank," said Nathaniel, cutting into his friend's flow at last.

"Fine, fine, it is your estate, after all, and I can't presume to tell you how to run it. So, you've been to Highfield House? Tell me, you wouldn't happen to know if Miss White has reconsidered granting me the first dance tomorrow?"

"Frank," said Nathaniel again, shaking his head as he turned from his friend. "You must stop this. You must stop trifling with other people's emotions."

There was a silence, broken only by a flap of wings over their heads. "I'm at a loss, Nate," Frank said then, with a little laugh. "Whose emotions have I been trifling with? If it's Miss White you are referring to, then I only wish she were in any danger of falling in love with me—however, she seems totally oblivious to my charms, and that might have something to do with the fact that all her attention is reserved for you..."

"It's Demelza," Nathaniel burst out, throwing up his hands. "I'm talking about Demelza." He turned back around, just in time to see a smile spreading across his friend's face. "For goodness's sake, is everything a joke to you?"

"No," said Frank, still smiling. "I'm only surprised to hear you refer to Miss Abbott by her Christian name, and I find myself wondering what the significance of that could be."

"Well, I'm sure this is all very amusing. We country people with our funny country ways... This is what you wanted to see, is it not? This is why you came down, to watch our little spectacle? Well, I'm happy to oblige at any other time, but not now. These are my friends, Frank." Nathaniel stared at his friend, breathing hard. "Demelza is my friend, and if you have made her any false promises—if you have made her imagine that you have any affection for her..."

"I think you underestimate your friend," said Frank, quietly. Watching Nathaniel, he reached out tentatively and put a hand to his shoulder. "But let me assure you, Nate, that I have not made Miss Abbott any false promises. I have only spoken to her once, and that was on the evening that we visited at Highfield House. She struck me as a very admirable young lady, and I imagine I struck her as a rather foolish, foppish young gentleman. Much as it pains me to admit it..." He sighed melodramatically, and then, sensing his friend's impatience, hurriedly went on, "I don't think she is in any more danger from me than Miss White."

Every word had been opening up new prospects in Nathaniel's mind. Now he felt staggered by the reality of it, as he tried to think of what other young man Gertrude could possibly have been talking about—and could only come up with himself.

Clara Seymour was surprised, when she turned the handle of the shop door of Johnson's, to find Mr Jorkins's maidservant on the other side.

"Ivy," she exclaimed. "Are you still here? It's late; I'm sure your family will be getting worried about you."

"I've sent word to them already, ma'am. I'm to sit with Mr Jorkins all night. Mr Thomas said he's not to be left alone."

"Of course," Clara said, shaking her head as though to clear it. She started forward, but Ivy was still blocking the stairwell. "Well—may I go up?"

"Mr Jorkins is asleep, ma'am. I don't think there's much you can do for him."

Ivy was standing still as a statue, but her green eyes were wide. Clara regarded her for a long moment, and then said quietly, "Thank you, I will be the judge of that. Will you let me pass?"

Another long, uncomfortable moment followed, and then Ivy turned on her heel and clattered up the stairs. Frowning at her back, Mrs Seymour followed.

There was a single candle burning in Mr Jorkins's room, and when Clara came closer to his bedside, she heard a sound like a whistle. It took her a moment to realise that it was coming from him: his breath was whistling through his nostrils at irregular intervals. The whites of his eyes flickered under his lids, and as she watched, they turned up and opened fully. His eyes roved around the room and came to focus on her.

"Why, he's awake!" Clara cried. Ivy was watching from the doorway, silent. "He's awake, can't you see? This is good news, isn't it?"

"I'm not so sure, ma'am," said Ivy, cautiously. "It might mean he's come to a crisis."

"Then call back the surgeon, can't you? He must be able to do something for him!" Clara bent beside the patient's bedside, seizing his clammy hand and pressing it in hers. "Mr Jorkins, can you hear me? This is Mrs Seymour. You must stay awake." His eyes came to focus on hers again, and he made some noise in his throat. "You must keep fighting this, Mr

Jorkins. We are all hoping that you get better: we all want you back with us again."

"I will go fetch Mr Thomas, ma'am," said Ivy from the doorway.

"Thank you." Clara did not turn, as the maid's footsteps faded away. Her eyes were still locked on Mr Jorkins's face. He squeezed her hand and made a noise like he was trying to speak again. Then, letting go of her hand, he lifted his own and pointed to the bedside table. His hand dropped again on the bedclothes, and his eyes flickered closed.

Clara stared at him for a long moment. She could hear Ivy downstairs, talking to someone. She wanted to shout, but she could feel there was something in all of this that didn't fit right: there had been something in the urgency of Mr Jorkins's eyes that sent a chill through her. She went to the bedside table, opened the drawer, and took out a notebook with a leather-bound cover.

"Mrs Seymour?"

Clara quickly turned, concealing the notebook in the folds of her skirt. Ivy had returned, but instead of Mr Thomas, it was Mr Quigley's valet with her. In the dim light, he looked rather pale and ghoulish. "I think you had better go now, Mrs Seymour. We can take turns watching him."

"Yes," she said vaguely. "Yes, of course. And you will summon a doctor?"

"Yes, ma'am. Your carriage is waiting outside."

"Good," said Clara, moving for the door. "I mean—thank you, Cecil. Ivy. And goodnight."

Suddenly she felt that she could not get out of the place fast enough. She could feel Cecil Simms's eyes boring into her back all the way downstairs.

$\sim$

Demelza had just slipped into an uneasy doze when she heard a light knock at her door. Her eyes flew open: it was fully dark in her gable room now. She had not seen Mr Quigley since he had locked her in there the night before: she had only glimpsed him from her window, walking with a strange gentleman. Cecil had come a few times, once to bring her bread and water and once to threaten her. The threat amounted to the same thing that Mr Quigley had said: she must keep quiet and mustn't cause any trouble, until she had learned her lesson.

In Bristol, Demelza had been locked up before as a punishment, sometimes for as long as a day. It was not the isolation which horrified her now; it was the knowledge that there was someone who needed her help, and that every second that passed with her here brought them deeper into danger. In school, she had had no one relying on her, except for her mother, who was miles away and beyond any help Demelza could have given. It was not so now.

"Demi?" A familiar voice came through her keyhole, and she sat up in bed. "Demi, are you awake? I can't stay long!"

Demelza rushed to the door. "Gertrude," she gasped, her voice hoarse from lack of use.

"I'm sorry, I don't have a key," her step-cousin whispered to her. "I just came to tell you not to worry, Demelza. I'm not going to let them marry you off to that horrid old man."

Demelza blinked away the tears that had sprung to her eyes. She had no idea what the other girl was talking about, but she was not about to say that now, when Gertrude was offering her help. She brought her lips closer to the keyhole. "I need to get a note to my uncle."

"To your uncle?" Gertrude sounded confused. "Oh, Mr Jorkins: yes, of course." Quick as a flash, she turned businesslike. "You must tell him about Cecil."

Demelza felt weak at the knees with relief. She hissed, "Then you know all about it?"

"I know everything," Gertrude assured her. "And I've told you, you don't need to worry. I'll write the note, and I'll deliver it myself to make sure it gets to your uncle."

"Thank you." Demelza's own voice failed her: she felt the tears welling up in her eyes again at her step-cousin's kindness. "He must know about the danger he's in..."

"Someone's coming, I've got to go!" hissed Gertrude, and in a rustle of skirts and a flurry of footsteps, she was gone. Demelza slipped back to her bed, fell under her covers, and slept soundly for the first time in two days.

Ivy Kent was tired. She was tired of answering doors, she was tired of watching a sick man toss and turn in his bed without ever seeming like he was going to die, and she was tired of lying.

Cecil had stayed most of the night; they sat up talking, and she dozed off against his chest. When she awoke, stiff and sore from sleeping in a chair, he was gone, and the grey light of dawn was leaking through the curtains and casting a long bar on Mr Jorkins's bed. He looked much worse, his skin papery, his breath rasping, and there was a line of foam around his mouth.

And then there came the knock from downstairs. Ivy rose to her feet with a groan and tramped downstairs, ready to tell off whoever it was, ready to deny them admittance....

Miss White was standing at the door, her face flushed with excitement and two shining black ringlets hanging down on either side of her face. She barely seemed to see Ivy as she handed her the note, saying importantly, "It's for Mr Jorkins," before flouncing away.

Ivy held the note at arm's length as she ascended the stairs slowly, her lips moving as she went over each word. By the time she got to the top, her eyes had blurred with tears, and she was trembling with anger.

Dear Mr Jorkins,

I hope that my note finds you feeling better and that you will forgive me the presumption of writing to you on no acquaintance. It is because my cousin Demelza is in a dire situation, and I believe that you are the only person who can help her. Her stepfather, my uncle James, wishes to marry her off to Mr Thomas. But she is in love with the valet Cecil Simms. Naturally, Uncle James does not approve of the match: I have spoken to him on the matter. But if you can find it in your heart, Mr Jorkins, to grant your niece the happiness of marrying for love, allow me to beg you to try your influence with my uncle. Yours faithfully, etc.

Gertrude White

Ivy Kent crumpled up the note and threw it in the fire before returning to her master's bedside.

After his long talk with Frank, Nathaniel found that there was so much on his mind that it was impossible to sleep. Faces and words flashed across his eyelids as he tossed and turned, and eventually, in the early hours of the morning, he had to get out of bed and go walking around in his dressing gown.

He was somewhat surprised, when he passed the library door, to find it ajar. Thinking that the butler must have forgotten to blow out a candle, Nathaniel stepped in and saw Mrs Seymour at the desk with her head in her hands.

"Mother," he said, groggily, and she sat up with a sharp intake of breath. "What's going on? You couldn't sleep either?"

"No," she said, with a sigh. "There was some... business..." As Nathaniel took a few steps forward, she covered whatever she had been working on. He took that in, and nodded, more himself than to her.

"I'm sorry, I'll leave you to it."

When he was making for the door, however, his mother's voice called after him, a little hesitant. "Nathaniel—wait."

He turned back. She indicated the chair beside her. "Sit by me. Perhaps you can help me with this."

Up close, Nathaniel could see that she had been crying. It had not been such an unusual sight, once upon a time: his mother with puffy eyes and blotchy skin, acting as though there was nothing wrong and expecting everyone around her to do the same. But over the years, he felt as though that had changed. Maybe it was just that he had had a respite, first at Eton and then at Oxford. She might have kept right on crying all that time, he reflected, and he wouldn't have known. The thought gave him a sense of powerlessness, and he suddenly felt that he had to speak.

"Mother," he said, as she drew open a black notebook and began to leaf through it. "Let me say something first."

She turned her eyes towards him, expectant. Nathaniel frowned, choosing his words carefully.

"I know that my father... did not care for this estate, or you, as he should have. But I want to tell you that I won't be like him. Not now, and not ever. When I come of age, when I'm tasked with running Hazelhurst and everything around it: I promise you that I will give my life to the work."

"I never doubted that," Mrs Seymour said softly. "I have never thought that you were like him."

Nathaniel shut his eyes. Weariness made him honest, and after a moment he said, "What is it, then? Why do you keep pulling me back? What are you afraid of, Mother?"

She sighed. "I'm afraid of myself, I suppose." As he opened his eyes again, staring at her, she added, "Afraid that I'll be shoved on a shelf again, just like I was in those days."

Nathaniel did not need to ask what days she was talking about. He had spent enough time listening to her sing, playing duets with her and longing to see the smile on her face that his music always brought. "You know that it wasn't your fault. All of those things that Father did—all of those people he hurt—there was nothing you could have done."

"Nothing?" Mrs Seymour repeated, with a bitter smile, and then opening the black notebook, she passed it to him. Nathaniel looked down at the cramped handwriting on the page she had pointed out.

"'Madras, 15 July, 1838,'" he read out. "'I received a letter today, the first letter from home in a long time—' What is this, Mother? Is it someone's diary?"

"It belongs to Mr Jorkins," she said, with a nod, and as he stared at her, she simply added, "Read on."

"'The letter was from my brother-in-law, Mr Abbott,'" Nathaniel read. "'He wrote that as he had recently discovered that he was ill...'" Nathaniel trailed off, looking up at his mother again. "Mr Abbott was ill?" As she nodded again, without meeting his gaze, he returned to the diary entry. "'... and wanted me to take over his business upon his death. He offered to pay my passage to England, so that I might be trained up in the position. I did not need time to decide—I took two sheets of paper and wrote my reply there and then and posted it. Poor man, I'm sure it goes hard with him to have no son and heir. But it is a good chance for me, nonetheless. I will hear from him, I hope, in a few weeks' time.'"

"He never heard from him," Mrs Seymour said, taking the notebook back from Nathaniel and thumbing through the pages. "Mr Jorkins didn't even know for sure that Mr Abbott had died until a few years later, when Esther started corresponding with him again after her marriage to Mr Quigley."

"Why wouldn't Mr Jorkins have heard from him?" Nathaniel said, frowning deeply. "Unless—Mr Abbott never got his response accepting the offer? Could it have been lost at sea?"

"Perhaps," said his mother, who seemed to be holding something back. She closed the notebook with a sigh. "Or perhaps someone made sure that Mr Abbott never received it. And who was closer to him, at that time, than Mr Quigley?"

Nathaniel shook his head. "It couldn't be." He had never particularly liked Mr Quigley, but the man was committed to his profession, and it was hard to believe that he would have acted with dishonour. But something else was niggling at his mind. "Was Mr Abbott really ill? I always thought that he died after a fall from his horse."

"I believe that he did die from that fall," said Mrs Seymour, quietly. "But he was ill. It was a great secret. His wife and daughter did not know of it, and I only knew because John told me. Your father was not very good at keeping secrets, after all."

Nathaniel was still struggling to understand. "But—how did Father know about it?"

"That is precisely what has been troubling me." His mother shook her head, wringing her hands together. "At the time, I thought it was because Mr Abbott's business was in trouble, and John intended to invest. But the letter Mr Jorkins received would seem to indicate that the business was still healthy, and that would have been at least two years before Mr Abbott's death..."

"And Father only invested after Mr Abbott died, when Mr White took over the business," Nathaniel finished, grimly. "Who stood to benefit? Himself, Mr Quigley, and Mr White."

"And who ought to have known better, and prevented them from whatever deception they worked?" His mother's eyes were full of tears again. But Nathaniel reached out and took her hands.

"It was not your fault, Mother. And we will make this right." His mind was working frantically. "Does Mr Jorkins still have the letter that Mr Abbott sent him?"

"I don't think so. It isn't as though I can ask him."

Nathaniel was too distracted to notice the tremble in his mother's tone. "Well, we must have more proof, before we accuse Mr Quigley outright. And..." He stopped short, thinking of Demelza. "We must tell Miss Abbott, too. She deserves to know the true circumstances around her father's death."

7

ASHES TO ASHES

Cecil Simms caught up with Ivy on the outskirts of town. The sun was climbing in the sky, and it looked like it was going to be a scorcher of a day. He tugged at her arm and, when she did not turn, dropped a kiss on her cheek. "Where are you going?" he asked, though the answer was evident, as they were on the dirt road that led to the Kents' farm.

"I've got to get changed," she said, her eyes fixed on the road. Her entire demeanour was off. Cecil thought he knew the reason.

"Listen, I'm sorry I left you alone with Jorkins. I know I said I'd stay till morning, but I had something to do." Cecil tugged her towards him again, looping an arm around her shoulders. She allowed the embrace, grudgingly. "Come on, Ivy, don't be angry with me. Don't you want to know where I've been?"

She was silent. Cecil let his arm drop to her waist, pulling her closer to his side. "I've been to see about getting us a wedding licence. Don't you see, with the money Mr Quigley's going to give us, we'll have enough to get us started? We can get out of this place, go north to Manchester, maybe. I hear there's good work there in the factories—work that pays a lot better than scrubbing floors or ironing shirts, anyway. Or..." Seeing that she was still silent, "Or we can go wherever you'd like to go, Ivy. Just say the word."

They had reached a stile, and Ivy broke free from his hold so that she could climb it. Cecil went after her, and when they got into the field, she turned right around to face him. She was not smiling. "Do you want to marry me?"

"Of course, I do," he spluttered. "I just asked you, didn't I?"

"Do you love me?" Her bold green eyes were steady on his.

"Of course, I do! I've told you enough times, haven't I?"

Ivy considered this, and then reached out and slapped him in the face. Cecil spluttered in disbelief as he overbalanced and fell in the mud. "What—what..."

"I don't believe anything you say, Cecil Simms," she snapped. "And I never want to see you again."

"Ivy—Ivy!" Cecil shouted after her as she walked away. "You little harpy, you've just ruined my best shirt! Ivy, come back!"

Demelza had been awake for some time, listening to the familiar sound of the church bells. The sky through her gable window was cornflower blue, and shafts of sunlight ran around her room, highlighting the dust motes that floated in the air. She jumped up as soon as she heard the key in the lock.

"Well," said Gertrude, as she came in, with a smile. She was still in her outdoor clothes.

"Well?" said Demelza, eagerly. "Did you manage to get the note to my uncle?"

"I did. Come on, get dressed; Mrs White has sent me up to help you get ready."

"To help me? Why?"

"Yes, well, we have a very important guest." Gertrude regarded Demelza with some sympathy. "I suppose you are going to have to meet him—that horrid man, Mr Thomas. But don't worry, as soon as your uncle talks to Mr Quigley, I'm sure he's bound to give you and Cecil permission."

Demelza, who had her nightdress halfway over her head, froze; Gertrude came and helped her get the rest of it off. "Me and Cecil? Whatever do you mean?"

"No need to be coy now, Miss Demi," said Gertrude, turning toward Demelza's wardrobe with a knowing smile. "Now, have you anything that isn't black? I have orders that you're supposed to wear something colourful." She drew out a grey silk dress.

"But that's my best one," Demelza said, faintly. "I was saving it for the ball—though I'm not likely to be able to go now."

"No," agreed Gertrude. "I suppose it depends on how long Uncle James wants to punish you. Though at least it means you won't have to be away from Cecil."

"Gertrude." Demelza eyed the other girl warily. "If this is some sort of joke, I don't find it very funny."

"Joke? Why would I joke about something like that?" Coming forward, Gertrude handed her the dress, with a thoughtful air. "I think you're so brave, Demi. I really do admire you. And I suppose there isn't such a difference in your positions. Not so much that it should matter, anyway..."

"Gertrude." Demelza put the dress aside and folded her arms over her shift. "Do you think that I'm in love with Cecil?"

"Do I think it? I know it! Why else would you have asked me to send that note to your uncle? And don't think I haven't noticed all your secret looks, your clandestine meetings..."

"Gertrude," said Demelza again, in the same firm tone of voice. "I am not in love with Cecil. I thought that you agreed to send that note because you knew what I knew."

"And what is that?" The other girl's voice was sceptical; the smile had dropped from her face.

"That Cecil has been planning something underhanded with Mr Quigley," Demelza said, lowering her voice. "Something to do with my uncle! And the maidservant knows about it, too, I caught her and Cecil talking about it last week, and just yesterday Cecil threatened me not to speak of it—that's why I was locked away here! I thought you knew..."

"You're lying," said Gertrude. She drew back from her, without dropping her eyes from Demelza's. "And I must have been a fool, helping you—feeling sorry for you! They're all right about you: Mother, Aunt Agnes, everyone. You're nothing but trouble. You're jealous of me, and you hate Uncle James for marrying your mother, and that's why you made all these things up! Well, don't think I'm going to feel sorry for you this time."

She went out and slammed the door. Demelza took a few staggering steps back and sat down hard on her bed.

～

Downstairs in the drawing room, Demelza was greeted with the sight of a broad-chested, bow-legged man with a grey moustache. He turned toward her with a surprised smile.

"Demelza," said Mr Quigley, who was standing off to the side, "this is Percival Thomas, the surgeon who has been attending your uncle. Percy, this is my stepdaughter Demelza."

"How is my uncle?" Demelza burst out, as soon as she had shaken hands with the man (his grip was so strong that she felt a buzzing all the way up her arm when he had let go). "I haven't seen him in days—I..." Her eyes slipped toward Mr Quigley, who was watching her with a neutral expression. "I have been confined to my room."

"She's much nicer than I was expecting," said Mr Thomas to Mr Quigley, ignoring her question. "Why, I was picturing a little harridan, the way you described her." His eyes flicked back to Demelza, looking her up and down. "But she looks nice and neat. What age is she?"

"Seventeen," said Mr Quigley. "I fear she might give you a little trouble at first, though. You will have to discipline her."

The door opened behind them, and Demelza, whose eyes had been passing back and forth between the two men, leapt backward in relief, clutching at the older woman's arm. "Mrs White!"

"Now, Demelza, I have told you before to call me Aunt Josephine," said Mrs White, calmly, without looking at her. "Percival, you mustn't be offended by her behaviour. She is easily spooked, you know."

"Like a thoroughbred horse," said Mr Quigley, with a strange contortion of his face, which Demelza realised a moment later, was a grin.

"Then," said Mr Thomas, raising his eyebrows significantly, "then I suppose I shall have to break her in."

All three of them laughed. Demelza felt frozen to the spot. She wondered, desperately, if she was still asleep. She could not be awake: this could not be happening. She let out an involuntary cry and started backward again, but Mrs White had tightened her grip on her arm.

"Really, Demelza, you are being very rude."

"You can't make me do this," gasped Demelza, her eyes on her stepfather. The grin had faded from his lips, but there was a feral gleam in his eyes.

"I think you know, Demelza, that I can."

"I don't have to live under your roof—I don't have to take your money—I can work…"

"You can work?" repeated Mr Quigley, as though it were a novel idea. "And how will you get a situation, when you have no money to travel to it? Who will you stay with until they need you? Whose charity will you have to fall back on?"

"I'll go anywhere," Demelza cried. "Anywhere but here. I'm not alone in the world. I have my uncle—" But she choked on the word, as she saw the look exchanged between the three of them. Her cry turned to a scream in her throat, as she lunged towards Mr Quigley. "You've killed him, haven't you? You've killed him just like you killed my mother. I hate you, I hate you, I hate you!"

"I don't think I like her so much now," said Mr Thomas, as she continued to cough out furious sobs. Mr Quigley's eyes had widened, and there was an ugly flush in his cheeks that not been there before.

"My apologies, Percy," he said, in a cold stiff voice, as he came forward to yank Demelza away from Mrs White. "Evidently my stepdaughter has not learnt her lesson."

Out in the hall, Mr Quigley dragged her first by the arms, and then, since she kept wriggling away, he grabbed a handful of her hair. "Stop fighting me," he snapped, close to her ear. "You've been fighting me since the day I married Esther."

"Because you're a bully," Demelza snapped back. "You made her miserable."

"Miserable?" Mr Quigley swung her around at the foot of the stairs. Demelza caught a glimpse of the maid peering out from the baize door that led to the kitchen, and then quickly disappearing again. "I loved your mother. I saved her—and you—from destitution and infamy—"

"We were happy until you came along! She had her work—"

"Oh, come now, Demelza, are you still a child? Don't you understand what was really going on when your mother worked at Hazelhurst? She was on the point of becoming John Seymour's mistress. That was why she came to me. I was a means to an end—"

"She was good to you," Demelza said, though her vision was blurring with tears; she felt small and foolish for not seeing it, for never seeing any of it. "And I think she loved you, in her way."

"She had no love to spare. She merely wanted to save her reputation." Mr Quigley paused, as though he wanted to savour every moment of this, before pressing on, "And, who knows? Perhaps she had already brought herself low by the time she came to beg me for my help. She was a woman of extraordinary resolution, your mother, but temptation does come to us all—"

"She never did! She was good, better than you'll ever be!" Demelza lunged at her stepfather, but he grabbed her wrists in an iron grip. Slowly, painfully, he began to bend them back.

"You have many things to learn, Demelza," he said quietly, as she whimpered with the pain. "You need to learn when to be silent. You need to learn that there are people around you who deserve your respect. I have taken you in—I have saved you, and your mother before you, from the workhouse. I have done more for you than most men in my position would do..."

"Please—"

"And I will not be insulted in front of my friends and family: I will not have baseless accusations thrown at me from your spiteful, ungrateful lips—"

"Stop, stop, for heaven's sake, stop!"

Gertrude had come between them; Demelza was released and fell back into her supporting arms with a cry of relief. Mr Quigley's hands were still raised, he was breathing hard as he turned his gaze to his niece. "Stay out of this, Gertrude."

"I won't let you hurt her," Gertrude said calmly, her arm still around Demelza. Mr Quigley's dark eyes narrowed, and he reached up to adjust his glasses.

"Then I shall have to lock you both up."

"Oh, I should like to see you try," laughed Gertrude, and as Mr Quigley opened his mouth to retort angrily, she added, "Do you want to have to explain to Mother why you've locked her daughter away? On the night of Letty Seymour's coming-out ball, no less?"

"I will not stand this impertinence," said Mr Quigley, but his voice lacked the conviction it had had before; he cast one last glance at Demelza, murmured something about having to return to his friend, and left them alone in the hall.

"Thank you," said Demelza, as soon as he was gone. Gertrude let go of her, and cast her eyes over her, warily.

"Are you all right?"

"Yes—I—I think so."

"Good. Then get your bonnet and cloak and follow me, quickly."

"Where are we going?" Demelza stared at her.

"To town," said Gertrude, curtly. "To see your uncle and find out what's really going on."

"Then—you do believe me?"

"Yes, but you'd better hurry up and get your things, or I might change my mind."

The road to Hartleton was one that Demelza knew backward by this point. She had walked it so many times, stumbling with weariness. But now Gertrude was with her, striding by her side, without a backward glance for Highfield House. It was hot and dusty, but Demelza barely felt it.

They had been walking for about a quarter of an hour when the sound of carriage wheels made Gertrude stiffen and look around. She grabbed Demelza's arm. "That's bound to be them, coming after us. Come on, get off the road until it's passed."

They hid themselves behind some bushes (Gertrude made a face as her yellow nankin boots sank into the mud, but did not say a word), and kept as still as they could as the sound of the wheels drew closer and closer. They stopped breathing altogether when they heard it come to a halt.

But then Demelza peered out and tugged at Gertrude's arm. "It's the Seymours' carriage!"

They clambered out of the bushes, a little abashed, to be greeted with a liveried footman, who guided them to the door. Nathaniel got out as they approached. His pale blue eyes were alert and urgent as they met first Demelza's, and then Gertrude's. "Miss Abbott, Miss White, if you are going into town, may I offer you the use of my carriage?"

"What are you doing here?" Demelza exclaimed, and then, as Nathaniel looked a little taken aback, "I mean, how did you know..."

"I have just called on Highfield House and was told you were indisposed. Then I happened to see figures in the distance which I thought might be you."

"It's very lucky," said Demelza, earnestly, "as I've been hoping to see you, too."

"Come on, just accept," said Gertrude in an undertone, planting a hand in the small of Demelza's back. "There'll be plenty of time for pleasantries later." Demelza flushed and allowed Nathaniel to hand her into the carriage.

When inside and moving, the three young people stared at one another for a moment and then all began to talk at once.

"I suppose we'd better go first," said Demelza, once Nathaniel had made his apologies. She glanced at Gertrude. "Only I don't really know where to begin."

"What you need to know, Mr Seymour," said Gertrude, speaking more matter-of-factly than the other girl, "is that there is some kind of plot against Mr Jorkins, in which my uncle Quigley, his valet Cecil, and Mr Jorkins's maid Ivy all seem to be involved. They locked up Demelza when she found out about it and want to marry her off to a horrid old man. We'd just had a row when we got away."

"The old man is Mr Thomas, my uncle's surgeon," Demelza supplied. Nathaniel's jaw had dropped. "And what we can't understand is why Mr Quigley is so set against my uncle. I know that he and my mother... well, that they weren't..." She blushed.

"That they hated each other by the end," Gertrude finished. Nathaniel blinked in her direction.

"I can't help but notice that you are being very forthright today, Miss White."

"Well, that might have something to do with the fact that a man may be dying, Mr Seymour," she replied. "And with the fact that if not for my own blunder, he might have been saved sooner."

"It wasn't your fault," said Demelza earnestly, putting a hand over the other young lady's; Gertrude turned toward the window and did not respond. Demelza then hastily explained to Nathaniel about the misunderstanding regarding the note, and he listened, his expression growing graver by the minute.

"Miss Abbott is right in saying that it is not your fault, Miss White," he said, when Demelza had finished her account. Gertrude looked back at him, in some surprise. "Your slip cannot have made much of a difference, in any case. According to my mother, Mr Jorkins has been unconscious for two days now. He could not have read your note even if it had contained the information Demelza intended it to convey."

"Is he really so bad?" Demelza said, her voice hushed.

"His decline has been rapid. I am sorry, Demelza. I hope there is something we can still do to help." Nathaniel glanced out the window; they were approaching town. Gertrude picked at a thread on her gloves, scowling at his use of Demelza's Christian name. "As to Mr Quigley's motive, at least, I think I can illuminate you. My mother made a discovery last night." Gently, he passed into Demelza's hand Mr Jorkins's diary and related the tentative conclusions he and Mrs Seymour had reached.

Demelza shook her head, slowly, and put her hands up to her eyes. She did not appear capable of speaking, and Gertrude, startled out of her sullenness by the story, said, "So you think that my uncle Quigley is getting revenge on Mr Jorkins—after stealing from him?"

Nathaniel tilted his head, as though he were considering, and it was Demelza who answered. "Mr Quigley hates people who are weaker than him. He hated me and my mother for depending on him. He probably hates my uncle for being the person that he cheated out of an inheritance."

"And, no doubt, he knew that Mr Jorkins was mounting an investigation on him," Nathaniel added. "It was no coincidence, after all, that Mr Jorkins returned after your mother's death."

"No," agreed Demelza, quietly and sorrowfully. "No coincidence."

There was no sign of Ivy when they came to the haberdasher's. Cecil answered the shop door and glared out at them. "No visitors, I'm afraid," he said, beginning to close the door, but Gertrude stuck her foot out.

"Cecil, if you don't let us pass this instant, my mother will make you regret it."

"I don't answer to your mother," he replied with a sneer.

"Everyone answers to my mother. And we're coming in whether you like it or not." Gertrude shouldered her way in, and Demelza followed. Nathaniel was last, and he kept Cecil ahead of him, anxious not to let the valet out of his sight.

The smell of the sickroom was overpowering, and the curtains were half-closed so that only a yellow light pervaded the air. "What on earth," muttered Nathaniel, as he looked around. Mr Jorkins lay on his bed, so still that but for the odd raspy whistle of breath, they might have thought he was dead already.

"Well, it's little wonder he's not getting better, in a room like this," Gertrude exclaimed. "What have you been doing to him, Cecil?"

The valet was hovering in the doorway and shrugged off the question. "I haven't been doing anything."

"What do you mean?" said Demelza, sharply. She had been staring at Mr Jorkins's bed, and now turned that blank stare on Cecil. "What do you mean, you haven't been doing anything?"

"It's that man," said Gertrude, eyes wide. "That horrid old man. He's been 'attending' Mr Jorkins for the past two days. He's my uncle's friend, after all, isn't he? Why didn't we think of it before?"

"Then there's only one thing to do," Nathaniel declared. "I'm going to the magistrate's office—and you're coming with me, Simms," he added to Cecil, catching him by the arm as he was about to slip out the doorway. "Miss White, can you fetch a surgeon? A real one?"

"Certainly," said Gertrude, with a proud tilt of her head, and Demelza, feeling Nathaniel's indecision as he regarded her, hurriedly said,

"If I may, Mr Seymour—can I speak to Cecil alone for a moment?"

"Of course," Nathaniel said, after hesitating a moment, and he beckoned Gertrude down the stairs. "We shall be just outside."

When they were gone, Cecil folded his arms and smirked at Demelza. "Well, well. You wanted to catch me alone?"

"Where's Ivy?" she said, and the smirk fell off his face.

"None of your business."

"So you don't know, then," Demelza goaded.

"I do know." Cecil flared up. "She's gone back to the farm. She's angry at me for something, I don't know what."

"I might have an idea," said Demelza quietly, more to herself than to him.

Outside, she said to Nathaniel, "I can take a message to your mother at the Grange, to tell her what is going on."

He lit up, turning to her in gratitude. "Yes, thank you, Demelza. She is making preparations for Letty's ball, so she could not come with me. You must use the carriage and take care."

They were about to split off to go their separate ways when Gertrude took Demelza aside.

"I want you to know, Demi," she said, with her eyes on Nathaniel's retreating back, "that I haven't given up."

Demelza blinked. "And before you can call me callous," Gertrude carried on, "To bring it up at a time like this, let me remind you: this is important to me. He is important to me."

"He's important to me, too," said Demelza, meeting the taller girl's eyes. "I've known him since I was a child."

"But I know him better." Gertrude suddenly seemed so sure of herself that it was impossible not to feel disheartened in the sweep of her gaze. "And I would be better for him, Demelza: you must know it in your heart."

Demelza felt very strange travelling in Nathaniel's carriage back to Hazelhurst Grange. She felt even stranger asking the driver to stop outside the Kents' farm, so she could not help but wonder if what Gertrude had said was true: if she would be really suited to this role. However, there was no time to dwell on that: no time to dwell on the sinking feeling within her, for she had seen her uncle pale and motionless in his bed, and she knew that someone had to answer for it.

Robbie Kent was pushing a wheelbarrow through the yard around the side of the farmhouse, and grinned when he saw Demelza, pushing up his cap. "Hullo! Are you still afraid of dogs?" Without waiting for her response, he whistled, and a collie came bounding out of the barn to run headlong into Demelza.

She bent, patting the dog tentatively as it wriggled and writhed for attention. "Scratch under her chin," Robbie advised. "She likes that." Demelza obeyed, kneeling down and trying to keep the dog's muzzle away from her dress, without much success.

"Where's your sister?" she asked Robbie, still patting absent-mindedly; the dog rolled over to try to regain her attention.

"Hiding," said the boy, with a shrug, and they both looked towards the farmhouse just in time to see a pale face disappear from the window. "She's in trouble, isn't she?"

Demelza did not reply to that, just kept scratching the dog's ears. "I hope you're keeping out of trouble."

"I haven't been back to the Grange, anyway. I wasn't likely to, after the lashing Dad gave me. Anyway, I've been helping him out here since. He..." Robbie paused as a distant shout echoed across the fields towards them. "Better run." He shoved the wheelbarrow into a corner and bounded off, the dog leaping after him.

"What do you want?"

Demelza, a smile still lingering on her face, turned to the kitchen door to find Ivy watching her. The girl was drying a plate on her apron, and affecting an air of indifference; her eyes, however, were rimmed with red, and filled with burning dislike.

"May I come in?" said Demelza, and when the girl shrugged, she followed her into a small, cluttered kitchen. Something was bubbling on the stove, in a chipped pot, and two girls on the floor were going over their letters. The light that filtered in through the dingy, cracked windows was dingy itself, daylight filtered through a layer of grime.

"Clear out," Ivy told the girls, and stood at the stove when they had left, crossing her arms as she looked at Demelza. "Well?"

"I've come to ask you to do the right thing," said Demelza, gently.

"And what's that?"

"Tell people about Mr Quigley, about what he got you and Cecil to do." As Ivy scoffed, "You're an important witness: you're probably our only witness, since Cecil probably isn't going to say anything."

"And what makes you think that?" Ivy demanded.

"He's too loyal to Mr Quigley," Demelza said evenly. "It's all he cares about."

"Oh, then you know him better than I do, I suppose." Ivy lifted the spoon in the pot, stirred a little with a look of distaste, and let it drop again.

"I've known him for a long time," Demelza agreed, "But I've never really understood him. There's nothing between us, Ivy. You read the note, I suppose, that Gertrude wrote for my uncle? That was her mistake: she had the wrong idea about Cecil and me."

Ivy said nothing. Demelza continued, after a moment's pause, "But maybe it wasn't a wrong idea to get away from him, Ivy. Because I think that maybe he can't love anyone as much as he loves himself."

"Thought you said you didn't understand him," Ivy said, levelling a suspicious glance in Demelza's direction.

"I didn't, at first, but I think I'm starting to. I think Mr Quigley's also like that." Demelza took a step forward. "But we're different, Ivy. We feel things: we feel sorry for people, we feel guilty when we've done wrong, we feel love for people even when they have disappointed us."

Ivy's expression as she looked down at the cooking pot was suddenly so intense that Demelza thought she might be holding back tears.

"That's why I know you can't carry this in your heart," Demelza continued, quietly. "That's why I hope you're going to help us bring Mr Quigley down. Because that man lying on his sickbed is my uncle, and I never really got to know him, and might never now. And I think Mr Quigley is to blame for that."

"I didn't want to do it," Ivy muttered, in a voice so low that Demelza could barely make out the words. She blinked quickly, and lifted her gaze to Demelza's. "I knew it was wrong. But Cecil talked so much about the money, and what we'd do with it, that I started to think... it might be nice."

Demelza nodded and gazed back at the girl sadly. "I think I understand that, too."

"Well, well," said Mr James Quigley, as he came into the library at Hazelhurst Grange to find a whole host of people waiting for him. "I must say, this is surprising. I was not expecting to be summoned here a full two hours before the ball. Is there some matter on which I can advise you, Mrs Seymour?"

"You are very kind, Mr Quigley," said Clara Seymour, from where she was sitting at the desk, "But our preparations are well in hand." Her son, who was standing beside her, shifted on his feet, and she glanced up at him. "Nathaniel will tell you why we have summoned you here."

Nathaniel cleared his throat, and the lawyer tilted his head, in a mockery of attention. "Mr Quigley, I have here some people who can speak to your being involved in a plot against Mr Jorkins: Miss Abbott, your stepdaughter, Miss White, your niece, both of whom have witnessed suspicious behaviour on the part of your servant and yourself. In addition, there is Ivy Kent, who claims that you bribed her and your valet to administer poison to Mr Jorkins. My mother has also recently discovered a document which calls into question the legitimacy of yours and your colleague Mr White's business.

"Cecil Simms, as I'm sure you have heard, was brought to the magistrate earlier today and has been arrested on suspicion of conspiracy to murder. Mr Percival Thomas, whom you arranged to attend Mr Jorkins and whose status as a medical man is under some doubt, has unfortunately fled town so that we cannot check his credentials. At any rate, Mr Quigley, we have called you here to give you a chance to defend yourself."

Mr Quigley, who had been listening intently, said, "Well, Mr Seymour, there is one charge which I can refute right away. I did not 'arrange' to have Mr Thomas attend Mr Jorkins; I simply spoke highly of him to my manservant, who happened to pass on word to his mother, your housekeeper. I suggest you summon her if you wish to corroborate that."

Mrs Seymour, without speaking, rang the bell, and when a footman came in, told him to bring Mrs Simms. When the housekeeper had come in, her face drawn with anxiety and her hands folded over her front, Mr Quigley smiled at her very kindly and asked her if she had, in fact, spoken highly of Mr Thomas to Mrs Seymour, and she confirmed that she had passed on the praise given him by her son.

Nathaniel, who was starting to feel that they were getting away from the point, cleared his throat again. But before he could speak, Mr Quigley turned to Mrs Seymour, and requested that she summon the estate manager, Mr Parsons. Calmly, Mrs Seymour went through the same ritual again. Parsons took longer to arrive than Mrs Simms, and when he tramped in, he still had mud on his boots and brought with him a gust of evening air.

"Thank you, Mr Parsons," said Mr Quigley. Turning back to Nathaniel, he said, "I must now note something else in this case which gives me concern. One of your witnesses, ah, Ivy Kent..." He imbued the name with as much disdain as it was possible to give a name, and glanced toward the girl, who had gone crimson, "is, it is rumoured, the illegitimate daughter of the late Mr John Seymour."

There was a collective intake of breath throughout the room; Demelza, who was standing by Ivy, squeezed the girl's elbow and glared at Mr Quigley; Mrs Seymour's face blanched, and Nathaniel, putting a hand on the back of his mother's chair, said coldly, "I fail to see, Mr Quigley, how such a rumour has any relevance to your own innocence—which, I must suppose, you are trying to prove with all this spectacle."

"It is relevant, sir, because you have called Ivy Kent a witness to this apparent plot engineered by me, and I must call into question her credibility, given that she is illegitimate and, therefore, not respectable."

Another gasp went through the room; Mr Quigley, however, had not finished, for now he turned back to the housekeeper and said, "Mrs Simms, I imagine that in your position, you must observe much of what goes on in this house."

"Yes, sir, that's right."

"Tell me, what you would say was the relationship between Mrs Clara Seymour and Mr Hugh Jorkins, before the latter fell ill?"

Mrs Seymour went limp in her chair. Her son glanced at her again, a deep frown creasing his brow; he did not move to support her this time.

"I should say, sir, that it was very familiar: rather too familiar in my eyes. I was surprised when Mrs Seymour didn't rebuke Mr Jorkins for talking to her in such a familiar way. But then, she seemed to be equally familiar with him: when he first fell ill, I distinctly heard her recommend her family's doctor to attend him."

"And it is a pity that I didn't get him," burst out Mrs Seymour, "as I have no doubt he would have done a great deal more for Mr Jorkins than that charlatan who happened to be Mr Quigley's friend."

Nathaniel shut his eyes for a moment, his expression devastated. Mr Quigley looked delighted, and Mrs Seymour seemed to realise too late what damage she had done. Quigley called on Parsons next, who attested to 'secret looks' and 'intimate conversations' that he had observed between Mr Jorkins and Mrs Seymour. By this point, Mrs Seymour was red as a beet, and trembling in anger.

"So there you have it," Mr Quigley concluded, his eyes back on Nathaniel. "One of your witnesses is a testament to the indiscretions of the late Mr Seymour, may he rest in peace, and another of your witnesses seems to have indulged in similar indiscretions herself. In addition, since Mrs Seymour may have let her own emotions cloud her judgement in the matter of Mr Jorkins, you might imagine why it is difficult for me to see any truth in these charges."

"Take care, Mr Quigley, in what you say," Nathaniel cautioned, but his voice lacked the volume and force it had had before. Demelza had angry tears in her eyes; Ivy had hidden her face, and Gertrude was staring down at the ground. Mrs Simms, standing in the corner, had the slightest, almost imperceptible smirk on her face, and through the door which Parsons had left ajar, several servants had gathered to watch, exchanging looks and smiles with one another.

"Finally," Mr Quigley went on, as though Nathaniel had not spoken, "With regards to what may or may not have been witnessed by Miss White and Miss Abbott, I cannot speak for what my valet might do in his spare time. I believe in letting my servants live their own independent lives, you know, which may be difficult for—ah—others..." With a speaking glance toward the servants at the door, followed by a look at Nathaniel and his mother, "... to understand. But since, Mr Seymour, you have also alluded to their view of my own behaviour as suspicious, I would simply add my opinion that domestic disputes ought to remain domestic, and ought to be resolved in that sphere."

There was a confused murmur throughout those assembled. Nathaniel racked his brain; he knew that there was something wrong in what Mr Quigley had said, but it seemed that the more words flowed out of that gentleman's mouth, the more words evaporated in his own mind. He saw it all in Mr Quigley's smile: he saw that he had failed; he had let himself get flustered; he was a child playing pretend.

"So, Mr Seymour," said Mr Quigley pleasantly. "If you wish to escort me to the magistrate, I will go with you willingly. But seeing as not one piece of evidence against me has emerged beyond the testimony of witnesses of dubious character, I would suggest that you do not waste your time."

"The diary," Nathaniel blurted, glancing at his mother, who nodded and began to rummage in her desk, and then, turning to Mr Quigley. "We have a diary, kept by Mr Jorkins during his time in India..."

"I must stop you there." Mr Quigley held up a hand. "I draw the line at reading a gentleman's private diary: that is not the province of the public sphere."

"There is an entry," Nathaniel continued, doggedly, "in which Mr Jorkins refers to a letter sent to him by Mr Abbott, asking if he would take over his business upon that gentleman's death. When he attempted to reply to—"

"A letter, now," Mr Quigley interrupted, with an air of concession, "A letter I will accept. Have you it there?"

Nathaniel swallowed, looked at his mother, and then back at Mr Quigley. "No. Mr Jorkins has it in his possession—when he recovers..."

"Ah. Well, I do hope he does recover, so that we might clear all of this up." Mr Quigley spread his hands, as though in a gesture of apology, and bowed first to Mrs Seymour, and then to Nathaniel. "Until then, I hope that I have been helpful. May I be excused?"

Cough, cough. Cough, cough. Everyone turned, following the sound, to see a young man emerging from behind the bookshelves. He looked slightly dishevelled; his shoulder-length brown hair was flattened on one end and there were ink stains on his sleeves.

"Oh, I beg your pardon," said Frank, starting back as though he were surprised by the company. He was carrying in his hands a pile of papers. "I must have fallen asleep while I was studying."

Mr Quigley raised his white eyebrows and exchanged an amused glance with Mrs Simms and Parsons. Nathaniel gritted his teeth and felt, in that moment, that he could have killed his friend. And then Frank Honeychurch's eyes, fixed on Mr Quigley, shone with a sudden, savage gleam, and he said,

"Oh, but I am glad to see you, sir."

The lawyer turned back towards Frank. "Pardon me, are we acquainted?"

"Yes—well, that is, no, not exactly." There were a few titters among the servants, and Mr Quigley looked wearily expectant. Frank went on, "But my mother's brother and you, sir, were very well acquainted at one time, I believe. His name is Harrison."

It was a miracle. The smirk vanished from Mr Quigley's lips and the colour drained from his face, and, for the first time since any of the inhabitants of Hartleton had met him, he was speechless. The whole, sordid tale was laid out before the witnesses, some of whom he himself had gathered there, and Nathaniel was in such a daze of relief and shock that he had to ask Frank to relate it to him again much later.

They were in the gazebo on the grounds. Inside the house, the ball was still going on, but the dancing was over, and so the two young gentlemen sat in their dining jackets, enjoying the last touch of summer sun on their faces.

"James Quigley was a law clerk in my uncle's firm," Frank explained, twisting a blade of grass in his hand. "I would have been only small then, but I remember him when I would go to visit in Highgate; he was slimy and insinuating, and always full to the brim with flattery. My uncle, Mr Harrison, was unfortunately given to the occasional fit of intemperance..." At Nathaniel's raised eyebrows, Frank added, "All right, perhaps the fits weren't so occasional. Anyway, Quigley got himself higher and higher in my uncle's esteem, and eventually he tricked Uncle George. Made out that he had defrauded someone and had been too inebriated to remember. Quigley blackmailed him, and that was how he got a position in my uncle's law office."

"You never told me any of this," Nathaniel mused.

"Well, it was the shame of my family." Frank threw away the blade of grass and propped his hands behind his head. "Uncle George died a few years later. My mother knew that Georgie had been tricked, but she couldn't prove it. Until recently, that is, when one of my uncle's former clerks, Merton, was contacted by Mr Jorkins. Merton went digging for the documents forged by Quigley, and since I happened to be good friends with a neighbour of Quigley's, I was sent here in the meantime, until the documents could be found and sent to me."

"And the rest, I suppose," said Nathaniel, doubtfully, "was good timing?"

"Good timing and good observation." Frank poked his friend in the arm. "You didn't see me watching, but I watched everything. I made sure everyone thought I was here for pleasure—made your mother think I had a secret devotion to Demelza just so I could get a look at Mr Jorkins. If not for his letter to Merton, after all, we might never have had this chance again."

"No," Nathaniel agreed. "Mr Quigley would have talked his way out of it, if he'd been in any way prepared." He turned to Frank, with a sudden smile of recognition. "That's why you kept ordering things from town. You made me think you were an awful fop."

"And you nearly found me out when you went rooting through one of the boxes. It's a good thing I also like having good cravats and hair powder."

"Would that have been so bad? If I had found out?"

Frank considered for a moment. "I had to make sure I had all the evidence ready. The documents were being sent piecemeal from London, and I had to comb through them and make sure it all held up. Then, when I realised that Quigley was up to his old tricks again, I thought he'd better answer to those first, and if all else failed, his original sin would catch him out."

"So you're not such a poor student after all." Nathaniel nudged his friend, after all.

"And I don't have a fascination with provincial life." Frank gave a shudder as he looked at the rolling green around him, which made Nathaniel laugh. "The sooner I get back to London, the better."

"But you'll visit?"

"Of course. One of the young ladies here has captured my heart, after all; I couldn't very well stay away." Frank's grin widened at the look of concern on Nathaniel's face, and he reached out to pull him to his feet. "And that lady awaits my ready attendance now; she misses my witty conversation. We'd better go back."

8

AN ILL WIND

I t was with a comfortable trepidation that Demelza Abbott came to regard her new life, carrying with her always the sense that things could never be so bad again as they had once been.

Uncle Hugh was now her guardian, and his recovery was as slow and painful as could have been expected after his ordeal. They moved to a small house at the edge of town with only a narrow passage that led directly onto the street for a hallway, but with a small patch of green at the back where Demelza could hear the church bells as she helped their maid with the washing.

It was after Michaelmas that Mrs Clara Seymour came to visit their new house. The Seymours had been in London for most of the summer, for Miss Letitia's first season, and a weariness of city life showed itself on Mrs Seymour's countenance. She sat quietly with Demelza in the poky drawing-room for some minutes before venturing to speak, and then it was only to ask her what she was working on.

"Handkerchiefs for the girls at Mrs Aldridge's school," Demelza said, looking bashful. "I was supposed to make a set of a dozen, but I've started on the thirteenth now. I know it's bad luck, but it calms me."

"I think you've had your share of bad luck already," said Clara, quietly.

"Perhaps I can give this one to someone else. Would you take it, perhaps, madam?"

Clara smiled, surprised. "I would be honoured, Miss Abbott. Or—may I call you Demelza?"

"Of course." The young lady looked up, a little awed.

"I must tell you something." Clara folded her hands in her lap. "I blame myself for what happened to your mother."

"Mrs Seymour..."

"I have always known that Mr Quigley was not a good man," Clara continued. "Something in him, I believe, is... broken. As it was in my husband." She turned back to look at Demelza, who was watching her closely. "And your mother would never have married Mr Quigley had she not been in desperate circumstances. I ought to have helped her, Demelza, and I didn't. I am sorry for that."

"It was not your fault, madam," said Demelza, quietly, "What could you have done? My mother was proud. She would not have accepted charity."

"But perhaps I could have stopped John..."

"Mrs Seymour." Demelza sat forward in her seat. "It's true that my mother's second marriage ruined her. She was worn down by Mr Quigley, until she was so miserable and weak that she could not help anyone, even herself. She knew that I was unhappy in Bristol, that it was not safe for us in the school, but there was nothing she could do. Knowing that I was on the brink of death, and that she could do nothing—I think that might even have driven her into that nervous distress, toward the end of her life." She paused, risking a glance at the older lady. "You may not be as unfortunate as my mother was, madam. But forgive me if I say that I think you know something of that kind of misery?"

Mrs Seymour nodded slowly. They were both silent for a long moment. On the ceiling above came a creaking sound as someone moved upstairs. "You are very wise, Demelza, for a girl so young," said Mrs Seymour at last. "I hope you know that you will always have friends in us."

Demelza flinched inwardly at the expression but thanked the lady with all her heart. Mrs Seymour could not know, after all, that Demelza had once desired to be so much more than a friend of the family—or that the desire still gnawed away at her sometimes, even though over the summer, she had grown used to Nathaniel's absence and acquainted herself with the idea that he might bring a fiancée back from town.

Another creaking from above caused Mrs Seymour to glance up with an unreadable expression on her face, and Demelza took the opportunity to say, "I think my uncle must be up now, madam, if you wish to wait and greet him."

Clara Seymour hesitated for a long moment, her lips slightly parted and her throat trembling. "No, thank you, I must go," she said at last, and gathered up her things with a haste that seemed a little unnecessary, considering she had barely stayed twenty minutes. As she was going for the door, she turned back once to ask Demelza, a little distractedly, "But—ah—Mr Jorkins is well?"

"He is getting better every day, madam," Demelza replied, and Mrs Seymour let out a breath that was so quiet, it was almost inaudible.

"Thank goodness. We have all been so worried about him. We miss him very much on the estate." And with these stiff words, Mrs Seymour took her leave, and Demelza was left with the feeling that her heart was not the only one that desired too much, and that had resigned itself to a very little.

The mild September day had turned cold and wet, and Nathaniel Seymour was buffeted about by the wind as he walked along the wharves. Dead leaves spun through the air around him, and the waters of the Thames slapped up against the landing stage. He kept a hand to his top hat to keep it from blowing off and screwed up his eyes against the rain. Behind him, the skyline of London seemed to have merged into one large grey mass.

Outside the public house where he stopped, luggage was being unloaded from carts and taken inside. Knots of travellers stood here and there, some forlorn and some merry. A few children were singing sea shanties, others playing in the shadow of the clipper ship, with its acres of sail and massive hulls.

Nathaniel found Ivy Kent and Mrs Simms in the dingy parlour. They had just finished their dinner and stood as he entered. "Please," he said, waving them away, and would not sit until they sat.

"You're very kind to come and see us off, sir," said Mrs Simms, in a flat tone of voice. "We thought you were already gone back to Hartleton."

"My mother and sister have returned; I stayed on a few days to arrange some business." Nathaniel took off his hat and patted down his hair, which was damp from the rain. "What time do you sail tomorrow?"

"Seven in the morning," said Mrs Simms, exchanging a glance with her younger companion. "Though I doubt we'll get much sleep with this racket." The singing children had come into the building now, and a few of the adults had joined in.

"I won't be able to sleep anyway," declared Ivy. There were two spots of colour in her cheeks, and there was a look in her eyes that was equal parts forlorn and frantic. "I'm too excited."

"Are you happy, then?" said Nathaniel, carefully, "to be going?"

Mrs Simms grimaced at this, but Ivy looked at him seriously and said, "I know that I'm lucky, sir, that I would have been locked up if you hadn't spoken for me at the trial. But..." She paused and swallowed hard. "Australia is a very long way away."

"It will be a new start for you, I hope," said Nathaniel, forcing his voice to sound cheerful, though in his mind were visions of a tilting ship, tossed and thrown up between waves over weeks and weeks of sailing. He could not envy them, exiled from England's shores. "And if you should ever need anything, please do not hesitate to write." He turned his gaze to his former housekeeper. "We will miss you at Hazelhurst, Mrs Simms."

"Oh, I'm sure you'll manage, sir," she said, coldly. "It would have been impossible for me to stay on, as you know."

"Yes, I suppose it would have been." Nathaniel paused for a moment, regarding his hands before he continued, "It is terrible, what happened to Cecil. I am sorry that you had to experience it."

It was the first time he had spoken the words aloud, since Cecil Simms had hanged himself in his cell two months before; it was for this purpose, and no other, that he had come to see them, so that the knowledge of their sorrow would no longer gnaw away at him. But he realised after saying the words that they only made that sorrow more real.

"It was cruel, sir, I won't say that it wasn't." Mrs Simms glared down at the table. "And I don't see why he should have had to pay for his master's crimes."

Nathaniel opened his mouth to utter some quiet agreement, but Ivy spoke first, looking at her older companion. "He didn't have to pay for Mr Quigley's crimes. He had to pay for his own."

"He was always good to me." Mrs Simms's anger seemed to dissolve into tears, as her lower lip trembled violently. "All he wanted was to make something of himself. And he was loyal to Mr Quigley, just as a good servant ought to be."

Ivy put an arm around the older woman's shoulders and did not say anything for a moment. Her eyes flickered to Nathaniel, and she said, "You see, sir, it's never going to go away, the mark. No matter how far we go."

He thought at first that she was talking about the mark of infamy, but then Mrs Seymour murmured again, "So good to me." It occurred to Nathaniel later that Ivy might have meant something different. He reflected on it after he had taken his leave of them, walking back alongside the Thames that reflected the black night sky. It occurred to him, finally, that whether years or seas might separate two people, that spark of kinship, a chat in a rainy wood or a glance across a crowded room, was never truly forgotten.

Since summer, Demelza had had ample opportunity to reflect on the kind of work that she wanted to do, and one October evening, when her uncle Hugh was well enough to sit downstairs in the drawing room with a blanket around his knees, she proposed her idea.

"A school?" he repeated, regarding her thoughtfully. He had gained back a little of the weight he had lost over his illness, and his face was fuller, his dark hair neatly combed back. "Here in Hartleton?"

"I have spied out a building on Westgate Street," Demelza said, eagerly. "I inquired of the landlady, and she said I might rent it for three pounds a month. Of course, I would have to work as a governess for a time to save up the money, but then..."

"No, no," interrupted her uncle, waving his hand. "There is no need for that. I would help you." As Demelza looked at him doubtfully, "I have a little saved myself."

"But you are not working, uncle. And you are not going to go back to Hazelhurst when you are well, are you?"

"No," said Mr Jorkins after a moment, taking on a distant look in his eyes. "No, I think not." Looking back at his niece, "But never fear, Demelza, I will find something. I will not have you hire yourself out as your mother did."

Nevertheless, the next morning, Demelza got up early to write letters.

For those two or three families who had replied to her earlier that summer, it had been necessary to decline their offers of employment due to her commitment to nursing her uncle back to health. He had got a hundred pounds' compensation after Mr Quigley went to prison for bank fraud and conspiracy to murder. That would be enough for them to live on for a while, but Demelza's mind was always leaping to the future, to those days of uncertainty that lurked ahead of them.

She settled at her writing desk by the window. Out of mourning now, she had a new dress of moss green which crinkled pleasantly every time she moved. Her blonde hair was tied back in two loops behind her ears, and if she looked a little severe, that did not discourage her visitor in the slightest, when he peered into the drawing room and surprised her.

"Mr Honeychurch!" Demelza exclaimed, dropping her pen in her surprise.

"I'm not really here," said the young gentleman in a low voice, with a furtive glance behind him. "I've just come to give you forewarning. I've brought with me a very dull lawyer from London, who's got some exciting news for you. Now, I'm going to go out and come back in again with him, and have the servant announce us. Will you promise not to get spooked and run away?"

"I'm afraid I can't give that promise without knowing the nature of this news," said Demelza, with just the slightest hint of a smile.

"I've told you, it's exciting! Oh, you are stubborn, Miss Abbott." With another glance behind, "Well, I shall go and fetch him now, and I hope you will hear us out."

Demelza rose gracefully when their maid announced the two gentlemen, and showed the appropriate level of surprise as they came in. Mr Heywood was an aged gentleman with half-moon spectacles, who did not so much as glance at her as he shuffled through his papers and began to read aloud from one of them. Demelza soon found herself grateful for this lack of attention, as she scarcely knew where to look. Frank was pacing up and down the room with his hands behind his back, and she could see every now and then, when he turned his head, that he was smiling.

"This will was drawn up by Mr Quigley and executed by your late father, Mr Walter Abbott on 3 July 1838," said Mr Heywood. "In it, he dictates that in the event of his death, a sum of five thousand pounds was to be left to his wife and daughter. Esther Abbott-Quigley being now deceased, that sum belongs in its entirety to you, Miss Demelza Abbott."

"There was a codicil added later, in 1840, which left the five thousand pounds instead to Mr Geoffrey White," Frank interrupted, seemingly unable to contain himself any longer. He fixed Demelza with his earnest gaze. "But by analysing the other instances of fraud of which he was accused, we were able to determine that this codicil was forged by Mr Quigley."

Tears were clinging to Demelza's eyelashes and falling on her cheeks. "It's true, then," she whispered, even as every part of her was tensed and heart-pounding. "He did not leave us with nothing."

~

Nathaniel Seymour had been back in Hartleton for a fortnight, and all that time, he had been working up the courage to go and visit Demelza.

He had promised her nothing, but he had known for a long time that her heart was his. She was not the kind of person to hide such things. The hesitation on his side, therefore, was not due to uncertainty of her feelings for him. It was low and cowardly, really, and he knew it; it was a fear of the future, of what his mother would think, of what the town would think, of what the mistress of Hazelhurst Grange ought to do and be and say.

But his feet drew him to Mr Jorkins's house whenever he was in town, and he often saw Demelza writing at the window as he passed by. He wondered if she was happier now. He wondered what her future would be without him.

On the day that Frank arrived from London, Nathaniel finally settled that he would go to call on Demelza. It seemed inevitable that Frank would visit her when he was in Hartleton, after all, since the two were such great friends, and Nathaniel didn't think it exactly fair that Frank should see her properly and he should not. So he went with an excuse at the ready, of asking Mr Jorkins some question about the estate, and came up the front steps just as Frank and an older gentleman were leaving.

Frank tipped his hat to Nathaniel and said, "Don't blame me," before quickly walking on. Baffled, Nathaniel turned to watch them go, and hovered by the door when the maid asked him if he was coming in.

"Mr Jorkins is in bed, sir, but is happy to receive visitors if you want to go up."

"And Miss Abbott?" Nathaniel asked, turning toward the narrow stairs she had indicated but not making any move toward them. The maid looked uncertain.

"She is in the garden, sir."

Outside, sheets and pillowcases billowed on the washing line, slapping Nathaniel's face as he hastily brushed them aside. He came upon Demelza very suddenly; she was in a dress that matched the ivy climbing the walls around the garden, which made him realise that he had never seen her in anything other than black. Her friendship with him had been punctuated by periods of mourning, so perhaps it was inevitable that when he found her, she was crying.

Nathaniel, as soon as he saw the tears glistening on her cheeks, remembered again why he had waited so long to see her and speak to her. It was because he had known that he would feel this: this thing over which he had no control; this thing which was bound to cause him problems in the future. He had known that he would rush to her as he was doing now and take her in his arms.

"You're not to cry," he murmured as he held her gently, this tender, trembling creature. He brushed the tears from her face, feeling that he must have caused them and despising himself a little for the possibility. He did not despise himself enough, however, to feel that he ought to deprive himself of her. No, he pulled her more tightly against him and kissed her pointed ears and her white neck, all the while knowing that he was going down a road from which he could not return and loving every delicious second of it.

Fresh tears were welling in Demelza's eyes as she lifted her own hands to his face, brushing the freckles on his nose and the curve of his mouth as though they were dear and familiar to her. "Nathaniel," she whispered, and he remembered himself at last, and pulled away long enough to ask if she would agree to be his—now—forever—in the eyes of God and in the eyes of man—and she nodded.

"Yes, yes. Oh yes."

He kissed her on the lips then, and she stood on tiptoes and wrapped her small arms around his neck with a grip that was surprisingly strong, and Nathaniel was evidently enjoying himself too much, for he backed into a billowing sheet and would have fallen if she had not caught hold of his arms.

Demelza was laughing. He gazed at her smile and wished he could keep it there forever. "I don't want to ever make you sad again," he said, brushing a blonde strand from her forehead.

She drew in a deep breath. "Oh, Nathaniel. You mean you don't know about the will?"

He kissed her fingers and told her that he didn't.

"I wasn't crying because I was sad," said Demelza. "I was crying because I was happy. Because our troubles are over."

9

THE HIGH ROAD

The troubles of Hugh Jorkins and Demelza Abbott may have been over, but for the Whites, they were just beginning. With Mr Quigley in prison, the hierarchy of their family had fallen apart. Mr White took to gambling and drinking, spending more and more time away from Highfield House. Gertrude and her mother, conversely, spent more and more time within its walls. It was hard, after all, to walk the streets of Hartleton and to be met with disdainful glances and followed by mocking whispers.

Gertrude did not regret helping Demelza. She did regret, however, that their circumstances had been so painfully reversed; she could never have predicted that she herself would fall into obscurity while Miss Abbott only rose in prominence. It was difficult, after all, for a pretty girl to go unadmired, and Gertrude was pretty. She ought to have excited jealousy wherever she went, not scorn and indifference.

One painful morning, when she was forced to go into Hartleton to purchase material for a new dress (Mrs White, for the first time, had cautioned her to buy stuff instead of silk, in order to save money), Gertrude bumped into Demelza in Johnson's. The sight of the other young lady's new dress, black with blue piping on the arms and bodice, did not improve her mood.

"How do you do," Gertrude muttered, with the smallest of curtseys, and was making her way to the counter when Demelza stopped her with a gloved hand to her arm. She turned back reluctantly. "What?"

"I know that you may have your reasons for avoiding me," said Demelza, quietly so that the other customers in the shop would not hear, "But I should like to go back to being friends."

"Friends?" Gertrude repeated, without meeting the other young lady's gaze. "Why would you want a friend like me?"

"Why wouldn't I?" Demelza said, eyes wide. Silly little thing, Gertrude thought, couldn't even see her own good fortune when it was staring her in the face. "Gertrude, I've always liked you. And you were so good to me—you were brave, you stood up to Mr Quigley, you agreed to be a witness at the trial..."

"And where did it get me?" Gertrude demanded, in a low voice, for their conversation was beginning to attract attention. "You know, I think I shall never be good again, for as long as I live. It only seems to make more trouble."

There was a glint in Demelza's eye as though she might laugh, but when she spoke, her voice was earnest. "You know that you will always be welcome at the Grange."

Then, as Gertrude gaped at her, Demelza said, worriedly, "Oh—didn't you know? I'm engaged to Nathaniel."

"No," said Gertrude, as the room began to spin around her and the burning shame of being the last to have heard a piece of gossip set in. At least her cousin's admission meant that she didn't have to force politeness anymore, and she turned toward the shop door, her errand forgotten. "No, I didn't know."

∽

As the initial shock of the news wore off, righteous anger took its place, and Gertrude had worked herself into a towering rage by the time she got to Hazelhurst Grange. Nathaniel had trifled with her, after all, hadn't he? Everyone had said that they were going to marry, and then, after her family had fallen out of favour, he had never written or visited Highfield House again. How fickle men's affections were! Now he had turned to Demelza, and because she was foolish and weak, she had allowed it, even though Gertrude knew for a fact that he had been away in town all summer and had not contacted Demelza either.

All of these spiteful thoughts were running through her head as she got out of her father's carriage. But then she looked up at the impressive facade of the Grange and was struck with a desperate longing. Perhaps it was not too late! Perhaps Nathaniel could still change his mind, if he just met her again? She checked her reflection in the window of the carriage, patting down a few stray hairs that had been mussed up in her agitation, and froze as she heard someone clear their throat behind her.

"Miss White," said Frank Honeychurch, and Gertrude deflated in disappointment as soon as she saw his smirking face. He had cut his hair and looked marginally more serious than before. "I can see that you are as glad to see me as I am to see you."

"I am here to see Mr Seymour, and not you," she said, moving towards the entrance.

"I can save you the trouble." He matched pace with her easily. "He has gone to see Demelza."

"Of course, he has." Gertrude stopped in her tracks, racking her brain as she tried to consider what to do next. She looked back at the carriage and felt a little ridiculous.

"Might I suggest something, Miss White?"

"No," she said, but Frank went on anyway,

"Would you like to take a quick walk with me? Then you might convey whatever message you had for Mr Seymour, and I will pass it on."

"You want to be a go-between?" Gertrude regarded him doubtfully.

"It's a hazard of the profession, is it not? We lawyers are all go-betweens."

"Then you have passed your exams?" She began walking with him, all the while comforting herself with the awareness that since she had not agreed, she might turn back any time she liked.

"Yes, I somehow managed to read a book or two."

"You can pretend to be careless and ignorant as much as you like, Mr Honeychurch, but you forget that I was there when you exposed Mr Quigley. I know how sly and clever you are, underneath it all."

"I think that there was a compliment somewhere there," said Frank, with a frown as though he were concentrating intensely, "But it got lost between one insult and another."

They wended their way down the path that led through the kitchen gardens. Nathaniel's pointer began to follow them, his tongue hanging out, and Frank tossed a stick for him twice. The third time, he offered the stick to Gertrude, who made a face.

"Oh, you really are a fine lady, aren't you?" he laughed.

"I like dogs perfectly well when they are indoors," said Gertrude, firmly, "And when they haven't been rolling in mud all day."

Jack, running alongside her, seemed to sense the scolding, and turned his brown eyes up to her with such a sorrowful expression that Gertrude gave him a grudging pat on the head.

"Go fetch," said Frank, tossing the stick, and then he turned back to look at Gertrude as they entered the shrubbery. "Well? What message would you like me to give Nate?"

Gertrude reflected for a minute or two. She wanted to appear calm and dignified; no one could know about that half-hour of agony and fury that had followed her meeting with Demelza in town. At length, she said, "Tell him that he is making a grave mistake. Demelza, five thousand pounds or no five thousand pounds, is not suited for him. She will not be happy here, and really..." Thinking that she might well give a virtuous cast to her words, "... really, he ought to think of her happiness first."

Frank patted Jack as he returned, rubbing down his coat and stroking his silky ears. Gertrude stopped to wait, and after they had been silent for a minute or two, Frank looked up at her. "Is that all?"

"That's all."

"Then allow me to give you some advice, and you may take it or leave it." Frank straightened. "You may speak ill of me to everyone you meet, if you like; you may refuse to acknowledge me in company."

"Really," Gertrude started to say, finding his dramatics a little much, "that's hardly necessary..."

"I think that you're nursing your wound rather than letting it heal. I think whatever you felt for Nate, it's over now, but still you would prefer if he were not happy, because you can't see your own way into happiness."

"I didn't ask for your opinion, Mr Honeychurch..."

"No, and you may stop me at any time. Just say the word."

Gertrude was silent for a moment. Then, looking at Frank, she asked, "Do you think he might still care for me? Nathaniel?"

"I think you know that there's little use in asking that."

The dog was nudging at her feet again. Gertrude willed herself not to cry, as she let Mr Honeychurch's words sink in. She was not going to debase herself like that; she was not going to give him the satisfaction.

"What do you want, Miss White?"

The question startled her out of her gloomy musings. "I want this," Gertrude said, looking around her at the grounds. "I've always wanted this. And—" guiltily, "—and Nathaniel, of course."

Frank followed her gaze, looking toward the woods, the shrubbery, the house. "It is all very pretty," he agreed. "But for me, the same appreciation is to be derived from a picture of a pretty estate. This one rouses no special feelings."

"This one is the finest in all of England," Gertrude argued.

"And how do you know?" Frank turned to her. "Have you been all over England?"

Her sullen silence made him smile. "Well, that ought to be remedied, I think," he said, and then, with a new energy, "So you must agree to travel all over England and look at all the fine estates, and then report back to me, so that I can see if your opinion on this one has changed."

"Not all of us are at leisure to go on a grand tour," Gertrude said, pointedly.

"Well, then, how about London? Persuade your parents to get a house there next season. See all the fine sights—see Ranelagh lit up at night—go to all the plays—weep over Romeo and Juliet—dance with all the handsome gentlemen and break their hearts... There, you see? It doesn't sound so gloomy, does it?"

He had won, Gertrude knew, for she had betrayed herself with a smile. Visions of the future danced before her, planted by him, and she surrendered at last. "Will you be there, Mr Honeychurch?"

"Of course," he said at once, and then, leaning in just close enough so that Gertrude caught her breath, "And you may break my heart, too."

Perhaps she need not despair just yet, Gertrude White reflected, as the carriage bore her back to Highfield House. After all, there was one gentleman who still admired her, and whom she might very well begin to admire herself, given a little time and persuasion.

The happy young couple were to have a spring wedding, and on New Year's Eve, there was a party held at Hazelhurst Grange in honour of their engagement.

It was a modest affair, compared to Letty's coming-out a few months previously. A few families of Hartleton and the surrounding county were invited. Frank was not there, and neither was Gertrude, but that did not detract from the merriment of the occasion. Demelza had never felt so at ease in the Grange before, and many smiles passed between her and Nathaniel across the dinner table. When the gentlemen joined the ladies in the drawing room, Nathaniel and Demelza drew together again like magnets, and talked so much and gazed at one another so fervently that it was almost a little indecent.

Mrs Clara Seymour told her friends that she had never seen a couple so much in love. She was a little more reserved, however, when the time came to speak to Hugh Jorkins. He seemed to have his doubts about the match; she had noticed him watching the two often throughout the evening, with a troubled look.

"I suppose you will be sorry to lose Demelza," she said to him, and found, with surprise, that she seemed to have hit the mark. He bowed his head and nodded.

"It does seem rather too soon. I had scarcely got to know her." Hugh looked back up at Clara. "Nathaniel is a worthy young man, of course."

"And Demelza is a worthy young woman," she hastily replied, and then they were silent for a minute or two, the polite nothings evidently wearing on them both. Clara had already inquired after his health, after all, and she could not do so again, though she wanted to, every time her eyes lingered on his face. She had never seen someone pass so close to death and come back again.

"And of course," she said, wanting to distract herself from remembering those awful days, "our families will be often together now. You must stay at the Grange whenever you like."

"You are very kind, Mrs Seymour. I should like to visit, of course. And I will come back for the wedding."

Her lips slightly parted, Clara waited for more. His words suggested a departure, and she wished he would get it over with now and tell her. Seeming to sense her impatience, he cleared his throat and said, "I have taken a post as an estate manager in Yorkshire."

"Oh," she said, hoping her voice did not sound as shrill to his ears as it did to hers. "How splendid."

"Yes. I will miss Hartleton, of course. But I never intended to stay here long."

"Of course," she echoed, turning her eyes away.

"I am leaving in two days' time."

"How exciting," Clara said, automatically, and then they were rescued from the painful conversation as everyone got into place around the piano to sing "Auld Lang Syne". Nathaniel played the accompaniment, and Demelza hovered at his shoulder, watching his hands on the keys with fascinated eyes. It was very touching; that was the only reason, of course, that Clara suddenly had tears in her eyes. She sensed Mr Jorkins's gaze on her as they sang: she heard his soft baritone join the voices around her on the second chorus. She wished that he would go now, and never come back.

Hugh Jorkins was surprised, on New Year's Day, to receive a summons from Hazelhurst Grange. His bags were almost all packed for his journey. Demelza had been helping him, in between her trips to Westgate Street to supervise the building of the new school. When he was gone, she would have one of Mrs Seymour's friends staying with her, until the wedding.

So it was all arranged, and as he galloped across country to the Grange, he could not help feeling a little worried. What could Mrs Seymour have to say to him, now? Could something be troubling her? He had seen the tears in her eyes last night when they had been singing at the piano; perhaps there were other sorrows in her life, of which he knew nothing. In such a case, he resolved to himself, he would be grateful to find that she relied on his services as a friend.

But he found, when the butler showed him into the library, that Mrs Seymour had not summoned him as a friend. There was a desk between them, and she was all stiff formality as she talked about the cottages that had been built on the edge of the estate, the expansion of the Kents' farm, the new measures that had been put in place to protect against poachers... He sat and listened and nodded, and it was as though he was working for her again.

"You might wonder why I am telling you all of this, Mr Jorkins," Clara Seymour said at last, looking up from the list of her tenants to meet Hugh's gaze briefly, before flinching away again. "I am aware that you are leaving tomorrow. But I wished you to know that your work has not been forgotten, and that it has yielded good results."

"With respect, madam," Hugh said, "It is Mr Parsons who is to be credited with that work."

"You drew up the plans for the cottages," she reminded him. "And... Parsons is to retire."

"Oh." Hugh shifted in his seat, feeling they were in safer territory now. "Then you will be looking for someone to replace him. If you wish, madam, I can advise..."

"I want you to replace him."

He stared up at her. She stared back, almost defiantly. "Just... consider it for a moment, Mr Jorkins. Why should you go to Yorkshire, when you are only just getting acquainted with your niece? It is true that she will be married soon, but that doesn't you mean you must lose her entirely... she will have her own projects, she will need your help with the school, and..."

"Mrs Seymour."

"... and there is a lot of good that you might do, here." Clara paused, but only to draw breath; she did not allow Hugh time to interrupt before ploughing on, "My son, of course, is of age now, and to be married, but he will still require some guidance as to his estate. I can think of no one better to provide him with that."

"Mrs Seymour..."

"I understand, of course, better than you might think. Nathaniel offered to let me stay on in the Grange after they get married, but I said I would take a house in Hartleton, instead. I think a little distance is important, but it is hardly necessary for you to go so far away..."

"With respect, Mrs Seymour," said Hugh, finally breaking in, "Yorkshire is not so very far away."

"Perhaps not to someone who has been to India."

"No." He laughed softly. "I suppose that does colour my view of things a little. But Mrs Seymour..." He glanced back up at Clara, who was flushed now, her eyes bright and determined. "Mrs Seymour, I must decline your offer."

She shut her eyes, letting her chin drop a little. "It is not acceptable to me," Hugh went on, carefully, "to stay on here and be your son's estate manager, while you are somewhere else."

Clara's eyes flew open.

"How many miles are there, between here and Hartleton?"

"Ten," she replied, a little distractedly.

"Well, it might as well be the distance between England and India, if you're there and I'm here."

She was smiling, the slow, tentative smile of one who was used to sorrow and disappointment. "I hope you mean what I think you mean," she said, quickly, and put out a hand. Hugh twined his fingers with hers and brought them to his lips. Her smile widened. "Oh... good."

He let their hands rest on the table again, still joined. After another moment's pause, Clara added, eagerly, "Then, you won't go?"

He looked up at her. "I won't, if you promise not to go either. I don't want to be apart from you anymore."

"Me neither. I'm sorry, Hugh. I wasted so much time. I..." Clara trailed off when she saw his smile. "Hugh, it won't be easy for us, you know."

"I'm not afraid of a few gossips," he replied.

"Good," she said again, the gladness shining in her face. "Me neither." And together they rose, with joined hands. They passed out of the library, down the stairs, through the hall and into the blinding sunlight, and they no longer feared what was true.

THANK YOU FOR CHOOSING A PUREREAD BOOK!

We hope you enjoyed the story, and as a way to thank you for choosing PureRead we'd like to send you this free book, and other fun reader rewards…

Click here for your free copy of Whitechapel Waif
PureRead.com/victorian

Thanks again for reading.
See you soon!

LOVE VICTORIAN ROMANCE?

If you enjoyed this story why not continue straight away with other books in our PureRead Victorian Romance library?

Read them all...

Victorian Slum Girl's Dream

Poor Girl's Hope

The Lost Orphan of Cheapside

Born a Workhouse Baby

The Lowly Maid's Triumph

Poor Girl's Hope

The Victorian Millhouse Sisters

Dora's Workhouse Child

Saltwick River Orphan

Workhouse Girl and The Veiled Lady

OUR GIFT TO YOU

AS A WAY TO SAY THANK YOU WE WOULD LOVE TO SEND YOU THIS BEAUTIFUL STORY FREE OF CHARGE.

Click here for your free copy of Whitechapel Waif

PureRead.com/victorian

At PureRead we publish books you can trust. Great tales without smut or swearing, but with all of the mystery and romance you expect from a great story.

Be the first to know when we release new books, take part in our fun competitions, and get surprise free books in your inbox by signing up to our free VIP Reader list.

As a thank you you'll receive a copy of Whitechapel Waif straight away in you inbox.

Click here for your free copy of Whitechapel Waif

PureRead.com/victorian

Printed in Great Britain
by Amazon

28801862R00108